The Exquisite Rush

The Exquisite Rush

36-Minute Stories

By the Curators of the
Mini Sledgehammer Writing Contest

Indigo: Editing, Design, and More

Portland, Oregon

Curated by Donald Carson, J. B. Kish, Jeremy Da Rosa, Sarah Farnham, Daniel Granias, J. Turner Masland, Summer Olsson, and Ali J. Shaw
Proofreading by Jeremy Da Rosa and Ali J. Shaw
Cover design by Hana Hiratsuka
Interior design by J. B. Kish

ISBN:
paperback 978-0-9819422-4-7
ebook 978-0-9819422-5-4

Printed in the United States of America

Sledgehammer 36-Hour Writing Contest and Mini Sledgehammer 36-Minute Writing Contest are programs produced by Indigo: Editing, Design, and More, 917 SW Oak St., #207, Portland, Oregon 97205. www.indigoediting.com, www.sledgehammercontest.com.

To the many writers who have joined us
to shatter writer's block over the years

Contents

Introduction, Ali J. Shaw   1

The Stories

Not On the Syllabus   11
Jenn Crowell
July 2010

Never in Public   13
Fufkin Vollmayer
December 2010

What Money Can't Buy   21
Barry Netzley
February 2011

Angels to Nirvana   27
Blythe Ayne
March 2011

The Bicycle   33
Pamela Russell Bejerano
May 2011

Reality   41
Courtney Sherwood
August 2011

Cans   47
Elissa Nelson
November 2011

Eggnog Enchantment
Pat Jewett
December 2011

55

Jesus Comes Around
Lisa Galloway
January 2012

61

Dog Arms
Jack Mahaffy
February 2012

65

Beast of Burden
Jarrod Schuster
February 2012

69

Women's Health: Neither Here Nor There
Kathleen Valle
March 2012

75

The Proposal
Miriam Lambert
April 2012

81

The Quiet Man of Wholesome
Jennifer A. Gritt
April 2012

87

The Lake
Elisabeth Flaum
June 2012

93

Underworld
Elisabeth Flaum
August 2012

99

Dream Catcher
Melinda McCamant
August 2012

105

January
Kerrie Farris
January 2013

109

Cost/Benefit
Daniel Granias
February 2013

113

Forgetting
Pamela Russell Bejerano
April 2013

117

Bottling
Peter D'Auria
July 2013

125

Purple Pillows
Daniel Granias
December 2013

131

The Difference Between Snow
J. B. Kish
January 2014

135

What Comes Next?   141
J. B. Kish
June 2014

Milk Starring Sean Penn   145
Jeremy Da Rosa
January 2015

Burnt Ice Cream   149
Elizabeth Grace Martin
May 2015

Whiskey Ginger   155
J. Turner Masland
June 2015

The Giving   161
Sarah Farnham
December 2015

Parallels   169
Summer Olsson
January 2016

Stand In   175
Summer Olsson
March 2016

Extinction   179
Laurel Rogers
April 2016

The Disappearance of Bobby Gond
Donald Carson
May 2016
187

Only the Lonely
Donald Carson
July 2016
193

Baltic Avenue
Melinda McCamant
August 2016
197

Sanctuary
J. Turner Masland
October 2016
201

Terminal Encounters
Daniel Granias
November 2016
207

Author Bios
210
Acknowledgments
219
Event Information
221

July 2017

Characters: Writers

Action: Racing

Settings: Bookstores, cafés, and wine shop

Phrase: "Get it? Shattering writer's block?"

Introduction

Ali J. Shaw

"I *loved* that story," Sarah Farnham exclaimed in response to Donald Carson's "I'm not crazy about it." We were several hours—and several glasses of wine—into the first-ever Mini Sledgehammer anthology judging meeting. It was a long night of debating over which thirty-six stories to include and why, not to mention side tangents about proper prompt usage and the best balance of exposition and action. It was the beginning of the book that you hold in your hands now.

But that's not where the story begins.

"My idea is for an anthology of Mini Sledgehammer writers' best stories," Jeremy Da Rosa emailed me in early 2017. He had been cohost of the monthly Mini Sledgehammer 36-Minute Writing Contest, with Daniel Granias, for a few years by then, and the event and the hosts had attracted a talented core group of writers, not to mention a few new faces who came to try it out every month and often won. Not that that was the first set of regulars—there had been several rotations of core crews going back to the days when I first started the contest—but this was the largest and longest lasting group, and they were all interested in helping with the anthology. There were nine years' worth of stories by then, and a collection of thirty-six of the best thirty-six-minute stories had a nice ring to it. I loved the idea, and before long, the stories were blinded, the judging date was set, and the production schedule was drafted.

But that's not the beginning of the story either.

Rewind nine years to a rare sunny winter afternoon in Portland. My friend and fellow editor Kristin Thiel and I were having cocktails at Jade Lounge in Portland and brainstorming how we could build more community in the Portland literary world through our company, Indigo Editing.

"I like the idea of a write-in," I said.

Kristin paused. She was always pushing me to take events beyond the usual, to introduce a new slant, and I squinted at birds flying overhead while I waited for her probe. "What would make this different from any other write-in?"

I'd spent the previous weekend pretending to be dead in various settings and changes of wardrobe while my friends videoed their post-apocalyptic film for the 48 Hour Film Project. I'm not an actress—I can't even lie about using the last of the milk in the fridge—but I'd had an incredible time that weekend. I was part of a team, we had to use a specific prop in the filming, the director raced to get all the filming and editing done and deliver the finished DVD in time, and there was a screening of the various entries. I wondered aloud if we could pull off a writing event of the same magnitude.

It didn't take long for Kristin and I to hash out the details of our revamped write-in idea. It would be thirty-six hours long, from noon on a Saturday to 11:59 p.m. on a Sunday. People could participate individually, or for more fun (or, we learned later, sometimes more tears), they could enter as a team and cowrite their stories. We'd give four prompts that they had to include in every story—a character, an action, a setting, and a phrase (later sometimes swapped out for a prop)—and to get the movement element into the contest, the writers would do a scavenger hunt to find the prompts. We'd get our publisher friends and other iconic Portland businesses to sponsor by donating prizes, and we'd do a reading to feature everyone who finished a story. We were both glowing with the excitement of it—or maybe that was just from the winter sun.

"Now, what will we call it?" Kristin asked.

I don't even remember the ideas I threw out at the time, they were so unremarkable. After a few minutes, I nervously started wiping the condensation off the side of my cocktail glass.

"What about Sledgehammer?" Kristin asked.

"Ooooh." I was definitely intrigued.

"Get it?" she probed further. "For shattering writer's block?"

It was perfect.

The first contest went off with, well, many hitches, as first contests do. But despite all of those, we got sponsors, we got media attention, and thank goodness, we got writers. One Saturday morning in July 2008, Kristin and I set up our registration forms on a table in Northwest Portland's Backspace internet café, and writers trickled in to pay their entry fees. Three teams and three individuals huddled around the table. Then a fourth individual, clearly still in his pajamas, warily stepped up behind them.

"What's this?" he asked.

We explained the contest to him, and on the spot, he signed up. A spontaneous entry!

By midnight on Sunday, the writers were regaling us of their challenges on the scavenger hunt, their late-night story-development epiphanies, their squabbles with their teammates, and their nearly reckless driving as they raced to turn their stories in on time.

2008 was a humble beginning, but I felt an adrenaline rush with the community being built. Mel Wells won that first year, and we managed to secure her stage space at Wordstock, Portland's annual literary festival, where she timidly read "Moving On" and then smiled broadly to the audience's deafening applause.

Without a doubt, Kristin and I decided Sledgehammer was on again for 2009, but we needed to add more readings for the winner. And that's where the Mini Sledgehammer story begins.

We continued the Wordstock reading tradition, but we wanted a longer-lasting engagement with the community. We asked the winner, Alan Dubinsky, if he'd be willing to do more events, and a grin spread through his auburn beard. But, as Kristin pointed out, are readings really all that interesting?

"We could do an activity at them," I said. I think the epiphany dawned on us both at the same time: 36-*minute* writing contests. There would still be prompts and prizes, and winning stories would be published on the website, though we scrapped the scavenger hunt for the short time limit.

Alan hosted several of these readings and contests at some of our sponsor locations and his favorite cafés and bookstores. When the series ended, we got emails and phone calls asking when the next Mini Sledgehammer would be held. That's when I reached out to Andy Diaz, owner of Blackbird Wine & Atomic Cheese, which hosted a handful of other regular literary events, to see about having a monthly writing contest in his space. "Ali!" Andy's enthusiasm is almost always at a level of ten, but this was even higher. He happily agreed to give us the big table for each contest night, and he chipped in a bottle of wine as a prize for every month's winner.

Over the years, other businesses have invited Mini Sledgehammer to come to their venues— sometimes for special occasions, sometimes for longer runs—but the Blackbird series is the one that has stuck since early on. We still hold our monthly contests there, though the hosts have changed out a few times and the crowd size ebbs and flows. Meanwhile, the annual Sledgehammer

36-Hour Writing Contest grew in writers, sponsors, and prizes—reaching a high of over $10,000 worth in prizes—and we even began an online version so writers from around the world could participate. In truth, the annual contest grew so big that it became unsustainable and has been on hiatus since 2015. But not Mini Sledgehammer—that series continues with vigor.

Back at our anthology judging meeting, perhaps after another glass of wine, some judges started to stress about the fact that these stories are not polished to the level of stories you find in literary journals. They are, after all, written in thirty-six minutes. Would people want to read that? Should we edit? Should we let writers revise? Debate ensued, of course, and as we landed on the decision to keep stories in their original form with only edits to spelling and basic grammar, Daniel said he thought readers would appreciate that the Mini Sledgehammer process is "an elegant rush."

Yes, these stories are a bit rough because of the time limit. Sometimes you'll meet a character who seems important but doesn't turn out to be. Sometimes a prompt is included in the last line just to squeeze it in before the buzzer. But in every story, every thirty-six-minute opus, you'll find turns of phrase, interesting characters, and plot arcs whose literary genius may surprise you.

These writers have shattered writer's block, in true Sledgehammer style, but they've done so much more in sharing their thirty-six-minute stories with us and with the world. They've created community—at the events, on the website and social media as friends and strangers have commented their praise, on the side in the form of unofficial Mini Sledgehammer write-ins, even in critique groups that have formed among regulars. And now in this anthology. It's a community even grander than the one Kristin and I ever could have imagined back on that sunny winter day in 2008.

Read, enjoy, share. And if you're ever in Portland on a second Tuesday of the month, I hope you'll join us for a Mini Sledgehammer 36-Minute Writing Contest.

—Ali J. Shaw
Sledgehammer Writing Contest Cofounder
Portland, Oregon
July 2017

July 2010

After the first Mini Sledgehammers took place at various locations of sponsors for the main Sledgehammer 36-Hour Writing Contest in 2009, we finally settled in for a monthly event at Blackbird Wine & Atomic Cheese. We still held Mini Sledgehammer contests at various other venues for special occasions and short series, but the Blackbird series has been the longest running, and the majority of the stories you'll see, including this one, are from that event.

Character: A person with a unibrow and one eye
Action: Using a plastic milk crate
Setting: Behind a picture
Phrase: "Thanks a bunch"

Not On the Syllabus

Jenn Crowell

Behind the picture she's just pulled down from above her dorm room bed, the wall glistens with the sickly sheen of left-behind poster tape, its residue gunky and clotted. She rolls her own frayed poster up and stuffs it into the bright-purple milk crate on the floor, nestling it inside so that it joins a stack of CDs and a pile of books she will not return to him. Let him discover their absence, when he reaches up onto the bookshelf in his faculty office, ready to pull some obscure tome down, eager to recommend it to some fresh-man girl who needs her horizons "expanded." She pictures him scrambling to preserve his air of avuncular-et-flirty cool, and utterly failing, his five-hundred-dollar words baroque and over-compensating as a one-eyed man with a unibrow. His fingers will fumble, fishing out his back-up bibliographies; he'll pass them to the provincial newbie with a flourish. "Thanks a bunch," she'll breathe, before she knows better, before his own breath enters hers, before she winds up rolling her posters and stacking her milk crates, educat-ed now, but utterly weary.

December 2010

Character: A transit driver
Action: Surprising someone
Setting: A traffic jam
Prop: Sparkly wrapping paper

Never in Public

Fufkin Vollmayer

My breasts are leaking and it's rush hour in the rain, and because of the rain the Muni metro shuts down. We're in the big tunnel from downtown to the Castro, and Javier is just making noise. It's that gnawing noise familiar to every new mom, the kind that the nurse who posed as a lactation consultant explained to me, "See those little movements of his head and his lips parting? That's rooting." I stared at her dumbfounded, rooting as in, a fruit tree or bulbs in the fall? So she went on, "Rooting means he's looking for the breast, so it's a good thing."

Anyway, the rain has shut the tunnel down, and the overhead lights of the train flicker on and off, like a disco ball right inside the steamy, crowded train that's bound for the outer Sunset. Someone's got Chinese takeout, because I can smell it from here.

Javier is revving up to a whimper, and even though it's crowded, all of us packed in like sardines and damp and mushy, I am going to have to disengage him from the Babybjörn, undo my raincoat, and get my breast out. Out and in public.

Maybe with the lights going on and off like last call, no one will notice.

To the teenager next to me, who's silent and focused in some deep way on his iPod, I say, "Excuse me, I need to sort of elbow you to get the baby out." He stares at me, maybe not hearing. Or hearing and not caring.

He doesn't move an inch, doesn't even blink.

Now Javier is crying, and it's that piercing cry of the newborn, a bleat, a thin wail so primal and high, it's excruciating. Like some illustration out of the nursing manual, I leak into my thick padded nursing bra. Too late. It's gone straight through to the shirt. I start to elbow the silent, sullen teen next to me—"I'm sorry. Oh, I apologize. Shit"—and then as I accidentally hit him—"Please forgive me"—he spits out, "You cannot do that. No, you cannot. I talk to the bus driver. Right now."

Well, we're stopped anyway. Go right ahead. And with that, he pulls out a white earbud from his thick, black, skunk-head style of hair and pushes his way up to the front. We're not too far from the front, so he pounds on the driver's bulletproof glass.

Finally, the driver, like a teller at a liquor store that doesn't sell wine, only coolers and fifths and endless varieties of rum, she looks at him. She looks about forty or so, her brown institutional uniform, the one that I grew up looking at twice a day as I rode the bus to and from school, her uniform is shiny from too much ironing. The yellow letters and MUNI insignia remind me of a forest ranger. Maybe that's what she is, a forest ranger, and we're all the wildlife.

"She is doing something bad. Not right. Her, over there," and the teen who's taken both the earbuds out puts his elbow into his chest because there's not even enough room for him to give a full extended point.

The driver looks at me, and I dread what could be the inevitable breakdown. I know the look. Middle-aged African American woman giving me, the blue-eyed white woman, the once-over. All those years on her bus when, as a teen myself, all I ever did was to keep the brothers who followed me, sat next me, and knocked their knees into my thigh, and talked to me, "Oh, Miss White, what you doing? Lemme take you home."

Or maybe in my haze of no sleep and new baby and the lights dimming on and off like a metronome, maybe I am misreading her face.

The high crackle of the walkie-talkie comes through, and she picks up the radio and listens to the report about the flooding in the tunnel, "Uh-huh, how long? Well, we just wait then."

"So what you going to do about her?" iPod teen asks, again.

"Nothing."

Javier starts a full-forced cry. There are no other babies on the train, just big kids. Dark, I want the dark to return, because then I can pull a Houdini move and maneuver Javier out of the björn, under my jacket, up through the loose tunnel of my crappy shirt, and close to his target. Get him there—and judging from all the faces on the train, the people who might be staring—get him nursing.

"No, not right."

"Actually, it's a public place."

I smile and nod and shove Javier on to my boob, and the moment we've all been waiting for, the latch, it happens.

We're in the dark, and the closely calibrated trains, they're all piling up. It's gridlock in the tunnel as two trains in a row, with big round headlights, a full moon illuminating the pitch-black darkness of the tunnel with no light, no light at all, the full moons are lighting them up. There's a traffic jam, and it's completely silent.

The pneumatics of the door exhale as the driver sits there. The teen next to me sits down again and bumps my arm, and I'd totally forgotten about the package wrapped in crinkly wrapping paper that I'd shoved into my backpack, the birthday present for Granny Doe, the one I'd dragged little Javier out in the rain, out of his cocoon, to Macy's, all to buy Granny Doe some plates to match her set from her wedding.

The driver now gets up and comes down the aisle to avert the panic. "There's flooding in the tunnel, a backup with an accident on the line outside. We'll be moving in about ten minutes."

As she passes me, she looks down and looks at me and stares. "Well hello, Karen. Long time."

"Excuse me?"

"How ya doin'?"

I stare and again that bovine look of stupidity must be overtaking my face, the one caused by exhaustion.

"It's me. Deborah."

"From Lowell?"

And she starts laughing and nodding her head, and all the backstory that wound through the short fuse known as my brain vanishes.

"Yeah, you got it."

"Hey. Hey, Deborah."

We looked at each other, right in the eyes. Deborah, who I went to Lowell with. Deborah, who smoked pot with me down in the pit. Who brought her plaid Thermos full of milk and bourbon to school. We used to laugh and laugh—could've been the pot, could've been finally figuring out the George Clinton's liner notes, *Some of My Best Friends Are Jokes*.

We laughed, and Javier nursed, and the lights came back and stayed on.

February 2011

Character: A wedding planner
Action: Putting on the oxygen mask
Setting: On an airplane
Phrase: "I'm allergic"

What Money Can't Buy

Barry Netzley

Being rich is a mixed bag. I know you're all thinking, "Yeah, right!" and I understand how you feel. The problem with being rich is that you have the money to do, basically, whatever you want, so there is this pressure to actually do it. More specifically, you're often pressured to do what everyone else says you want.

After I proposed, my bride to be, Sandy, picked New Zealand for our wedding and honeymoon. I live in Utah for good reason: it's mostly flat, there are few bodies of water, no hurricanes, no tornadoes, earthquakes are rare, and you can go anywhere you want in your very own car.

"Sandy! What are you thinking? I can't go to New Zealand. Are you crazy?"

Sandy was not about to give me any slack. She had thought this out; she had a plan. Tough Love was to be her wedding theme. "Why can't you, babe?" she cooed. "It's just a plane."

"Because I'm allergic!" I yelled.

"Allergic to what?"

"To everything!"

Cue the wedding planner and the life coach and the couples counselor and the hypnotist. Cue the mock airplane. Throwing money at the problem, Qantas delivered a shiny 747 flight trainer, and every day for a month, our whole crew gathered. We trained and trained and trained.

Just climbing the ladder and going through that small door had me freaked out.

"Keep coming, babe," said Sandy.

"You can do it," cried the rest of the team.

"Remember the visualization," said Sandy. "Visualize a huge desert with nothing in it," she said, because all the typical visualization scenes made me even more anxious; oceans and waves and hawks flying and just floating on the water. So I visualized nothing but empty desert and made my way down the aisle.

"Row, three! Row nine! Row eighteen," they all cried. "You're almost there!"

By row twenty-two, I was on my hands and knees. I was sweating, cursing, mumbling to myself, whining; and they were all happily and lovingly screaming at me to "Go, go, go; you can do it!"

I made it to row twenty-six, way the hell back. It was like visiting all the levels of hell. I pulled myself up into the chair and began hyperventilating. The oxygen masks dropped down. I had the clarity, the urgent sense of survival to remember the safety video we had gone over sixty times. I got the string around my neck, the mask on my face, and I looked to the seat beside me, ready to put a mask on the child who was always there in the video, but of course the seat was empty.

And then finally, my mask began to fill, and I had the first sense that I just might live. I didn't calm down right away, but it was better. The wedding planner was rubbing my shoulders. The hypnotist was mouthing the words, "Deserted desert...flat...alone...safe..." Sandy was in the row ahead of me, her knees on the seat and leaning back to face me. Her eyes were like all the pictures you've ever seen of God looking down and saying, "I am love. You can do it. You may enter the Kingdom of Heaven."

They told me later that they had spiked the oxygen supply in the customized flight trainer with laughing gas. I'm here to tell you, friends, that stuff works. "Movie," I'd drooled. "Where's my cocktail and peanuts? Get this baby up in the air and let's get cranking for New Zealand."

My first training flight was a smashing success. Literally, as it turned out. Descending the ladder, still unbelievably high, I fell fourteen feet onto the tarmac and fractured ribs, broke bones, scraped, bruised, sprained; you name it.

We spent our honeymoon, four glorious weeks, at a secluded vacation spot in the high desert. It was wheelchair equipped.

There's talk of California for our first anniversary. We can drive there in our very own car.

March 2011

Character: A women's activist
Action: Sneaking
Setting: A church
Prop: Mardi Gras beads

Angels to Nirvana

Blythe Ayne

I was crawling around on the church floor after my Mardi Gras beads, which had mysteriously jumped their string and flown every which way in a wild jumble.

At that moment, in the middle of the rowdy carnival celebration on the street, a bunch of women's activists came bursting through the door of the church. Don't ask me how I figured that's what they were—they just had an air of self-assurance and determination to change the world for better.

The first one came up to me as I squatted under a pew, gathering my beads. She stepped on one of them. It went *crunch!* under her sturdy shoe.

"What are you doing, sneaking around on the floor of the church?" she asked.

"I..." I gestured at the beads, green and silver and orange all around her. "My string of beads broke, and I'm—"

"Never mind." She waved to her compatriots, three other very sure-of-themselves-looking women. They formed a crescent-moon curve around her. Looking up at them, it was like a visitation. The streetlights came through the stained glass windows, making a halo around them. I felt like I was looking up at guardian angels. Gabriel, at least, for sure.

"This young man," she continued, "has broken his string of Mardi Gras beads. Help him pick them up."

The three women fell to their knees and scrambled around for the beads, under the pews, in the aisles...everywhere.

"How did you come to be in *this* church?" one of the women asked me. "Oh look, here's seven beads, all together."

"I don't know. I was in the street, celebrating..." I looked into her eyes. They were that kind of hazel composed of green and brown and almost red segments. I stopped talking.

"Go on," she said.

"I...you...your eyes..."

"I know, kind of strange, aren't they?"

"But I've seen you... Do you know me?"

She shrugged but looked away.

"Do you know me?" I asked again.

"Here's another bead." She moved across the aisle on all fours but somehow so gracefully, almost floating, as if it was a well-practiced dance move.

I scrambled after her. Clearly less graceful. "You know me, don't you?"

As she picked up another bead, I reached out to stay her hand. A flash of light passed between her hand and mine.

"What the…?" I sat back on my haunches, stunned.

The first woman came up to us, standing over us, disapproving.

"Just gather the beads!" she ordered.

The hazel-eyed woman moved away from me, picked up another bead, but didn't hand it to me.

"Give me the bead," I said. She cautiously reached out her hand, her long fingers stretched impossibly toward me, she dared to look me in the eye. The flash of light passed between us again.

"*I know!*" I fairly shouted. Then quietly I said, "I know where I've seen you. In my dreams. In my dreams," I repeated. "Have you seen me? Do you know me?"

She looked over my shoulder.

"Yes," she whispered. "Yes, I know you. But just leave me in your dreams. You don't want to bring me out into your real world."

"What do you mean? You *are* in my real world."

A saxophone player belted out a song in the street, a song I'd never heard but felt I knew so well.

"Just gather the beads," she said. "When you have 108, you'll arrive."

"What are you saying?"

"Count the beads—108—you'll arrive in nirvana."

I counted the beads, wanting only to look one more time into those strange, amazing eyes.

I counted 107 beads, then looked up, discovering that I was sitting on the sidewalk, under the saxophone player. He was about seven feet tall—his music came from far away.

"Hey..." I asked him, "Hey, did you see a hazel-eyed woman? An amazing hazel-eyed woman?"

He looked down at me and again, I felt like the guardian angel in the church window had come alive. He didn't stop playing, but he nodded.

Yes, he'd seen her.

The faint lace of dawn crept up the sky behind the saxophone player, pink and pale orange. I looked down at my hands filled with Mardi Gras beads, longing to see the hazel-eyed angel again. But I knew I never would.

She had kept that one single bead to nirvana.

May 2011

Character: A woman of a certain age
Action: Fleeing by bicycle
Setting: Between here and there
Phrase: "Don't take this the wrong way, but..."

The Bicycle

Pamela Russell Bejerano

Margaret stood looking at the bicycle in the shop. It was the latest invention—the front wheel large with iron spokes, a tiny seat atop made of wood, and one small wheel behind. She had seen many photographs of them, but this was her fist glimpse in person. It was magnificent.

"May I help you, ma'am?" Margaret turned and looked at the young boy, less than half her age. "Are you looking for a gift for your husband?"

Margaret smiled. She knew women were not allowed to ride such contraptions, but she also knew that this was hogwash. Women of a certain age, in her opinion, were young enough to be able to break such asinine rules and old enough to enjoy doing so. How little the young knew.

"No," she said, then quickly corrected herself. "Actually, yes. I am looking for a bicycle for my husband. But truly, you cannot convince me that these contraptions are not highly dangerous." She shifted her parasol from one shoulder to the other, getting a better look at both the boy and the bicycle.

"No, no," he said walking to the bicycle and wheeling it toward her. "They are truly safe. Watch," he said, stationing the bicycle by the mounting stand. He climbed up, swung his leg over the seat, and placed his feet on the pedals. "Watch," he said, then proceeded ever so slowly to move the bicycle down the road.

She watched him go, then watched as he turned the corner ever so carefully, and rode back to her, dismounting again at the stand. He smiled at her, as if it were the grandest achievement to have ridden such a thing between here and there, when in truth, here was there. Thoughts swimming in Margaret's mind were of a much grander sort.

"I suppose you're going to tell me I need to purchase the contraption to mount the thing as well?" she said, goading him.

"Of course not. It is just as easy to mount freestanding. Watch." He moved the bicycle away from the stand, kicked out a metal rod that held the bicycle upright, and proceeded to climb up the back wheel. "See, just as easy?"

"And this?" she said, pointing to the rod.

"Watch," he said, beaming at her. As he rode away, the stand flipped itself up.

Again, he rode to the end of the dirt road and turned slowly, then made his way back. How he would dismount was the only piece of information she was lacking. She watched carefully as he slowed the bicycle, removed one hand from the handlebar and placed it on the seat between his legs, then quickly leapt back and down to the ground.

"Simple as pie. Your husband will learn in no time."

"Indeed," she said. "And how much does this cost?"

"Well," he said, gently taking her arm and leading her closer to the bicycle. "This is not your average model. These spokes, see here, how they are connected at the center? That's the latest fashion, making the model much safer. And the pedals, see how they—"

"How much, I believe, was the question."

The young lad stopped and looked at her. "The seat, see there? It's fine Italian leather that—"

"My boy, if I have to ask you again, you shall lose my attentions permanently." She stared him in the eye, unmoving.

"Seventy-five pounds, ten shillings."

"Seventy-five pounds? And ten shillings?" she mocked, feigning shock. "For a contraption that will make one sweat to take it simply down the road?" she said, gesturing up the short distance of road she had traveled.

"Oh, but madam, think of all the places one could go!"

"Such as?"

"Well," he said, rubbing his chin and staring at the giant wheel. "You could ride it as far as, let's see..."

"Yes, just as I thought. An overpriced bundle of metal to get one nowhere." She shifted her parasol off her shoulder and overhead, turned on a heel, and began to walk away, smiling. She knew she had him.

"Ma'am," he said, running around to block her path. "Please, I assure you, this bicycle is sturdy enough, fast enough, it could take you even off to the next town."

"And where might that be?" she said, feigning ignorance. "There?" she pointed down the road she was facing that bent some hundred yards down into the overgrowth. A back road, she also knew, that led to Sussex, some sixteen miles away.

"Well, of course, though one would have to be highly skilled at the thing to be able to ride down that road."

"Oh, well, then," she said, turning the opposite

direction to the other road that headed out of town. "This way?"

"Well, this way, certainly. I've ridden there myself."

"Indeed." She looked at him with wide eyes, as if entirely impressed with his prowess. "I'll take it. But only if you can guarantee me my husband could reach the next town by that road"—she gestured down the shorter path—"on his first attempt."

"Ma'am, if I may," he said, looking at her. "Please, don't take this wrong, but riding such a machine will take some time. If your husband wishes to go over to the next town, it may take some time to accustom himself to the thing. But once he's done that, I assure you, he can ride as far as the edge of town if he'd so like."

Insulted as a woman, and by her age. It was amazing how well the youth managed to do that in one fell swoop. She smiled, thoroughly enjoying herself.

"If you would, please, then. I'd like to buy that one."

The boy turned to where her extended finger indicated. "That one?" he said, the look of surprise unhidden on his face. "But, ma'am, that's our deluxe model. It might be better if your husband learnt first on this one, then, in time, if he still likes it, he could come back and purchase this one."

"Are you quite through?" she said simply.

"Ma'am?"

"With your juvenile preaching. Are you quite through?"

"Uh, well, uh, yes, ma'am."

"Good, because you're tiring me. I want that one." Again she pointed to the larger model still in the shop.

"Right. Well, give me a minute, please. I'll be right back."

"I'm sure you will."

Unfortunately for the poor lad, by the time he was right back, she had hoisted up the folds of her skirt, mounted the cycle, and disappeared around the bend. Once out of sight and out of sound, she realized she had done it—she had fled her godforsaken life forever, and had done so in the most unexpected of ways—by bicycle.

She lifted her head to the sun, flew her feet off the pedals and out in front of her, and let out the most joyous, giddy yelp of her life.

August 2011

Character: A landlord

Action: Haggling

Setting: The set for a TV show

Phrase: "I just came over here to..."

Reality

Courtney Sherwood

It's not like I didn't know anything about the world when I ran away. Some of the kids in my homeschool group had televisions, and they'd whisper inscrutable tales about the world of sin when Mama left us alone doing exercises as she changed a diaper or kneaded bread. When I was very young, she even used to take me in to town on her supply runs. I saw billboards and the shockingly immodest attire of the modern world. Plus, Mama and Papa even talked about it, to warn us off, to explain why we lived this strange, sequestered life. Not that it felt sequestered. It was all I knew, and I was loved and nurtured and encouraged, as they raised me up to become a godly woman, a mother, a helpmeet, and a wife.

And it's not even like I was all that sheltered. The Bible's full of sin, and so are the lives of those who call themselves godly. Mama and Papa were kind, but some of the kids from our worship meetings came from stricter homes. No "spare the rod" for them. And after my best friend, Rebekkah, joined in holy matrimony to the godly man who'd courted her, I heard of other horrors.

Pain and cruelty that we didn't know the words for, and no way to escape. Marriage was forever, an eternal binding of two immortal souls.

Since I struck out on my own, I've met other girls and women who fled my sheltered, narrow world. Most were like Rebekkah—shattered creatures, nearly broken by expectations that they could no longer bear. But I was happy. It was the fear—fear of eternity with palm-shaped bruises, fear of a soul bound to a man I couldn't love. And yes, fear that the sin in my heart was greater than Mama, Papa, maybe even God could ever forgive. Though as I thought that, I cursed myself, because God could forgive everything. He was perfect. That I could think otherwise was proof of my imperfection.

So at eighteen, after Papa headed off to work and Mama left for her fortnightly shopping trip, I put my eldest younger sister in charge of the family brood, gathered my favorite calico dresses in a bundle, sneaked sinfully into Mama's spare cash jar and stole half of everything she'd left behind, and struck out east, hoping to have at least a few years of joy before the sin of it all devoured my soul.

I was book smart—I'll credit the home-schooling for that. I could read and write, do my sums, and quote the Bible on command. But I didn't know a thing about money or phones or work or the modern world. I slept outside the first night, and on the second day wandered into a town where I saw a *Room for Rent* sign on a telephone pole.

Took about thirty seconds of haggling with my first potential landlord to learn the eighty dollars I'd stolen from Mama was not gonna get me very far. That was three days ago.

The landlord was a woman, a lady with a day job and tall shoes and short hair, and a fast, important-sounding way of talking. A sinner for sure. Well, we're all sinners, I guess. But she was doubly sinful, to watch her move and listen to her talk, and not a bit contrite. So it surprised me when it turned out she was also a little bit kind.

"You really don't know anything about the world, do you?" she asked, the same look of wonder on her face as the young'uns would get upon discovering yesterday's tadpole had grown legs overnight.

"Look, you can stay in the room, no charge, until I find a paying renter or you find a job. Could be a day, could be a week, could be a month. But if I find someone who can afford my rent before you can do it, you're gone. And no pets, no smoking, no late-night parties, either." She smiled at that. "Somehow, I think the job part's really the only thing I need to worry about. You got any skills?"

I didn't know what to say to that. Skills? Though I can bake and wash and corral a horde of children, plus think for myself a little even, I'd never thought of any of that in terms of skills, and so I hesitated.

"Great," she said. "No skills. That'll get you far. Well, follow me. I'll show you to your room, at least for tonight."

The room had a big bed, a closet, and even a television set. I'd seen them before, like I said, at homeschool friends' homes, but I'd never turned one on, and that first day and night I was afraid to even touch it.

Day two, I walked downtown from my temporary home and went door-to-door in search of work. I never walked so much or saw so many strange things in all my life. Girls and boys holding hands. Men and women with skin all different colors. So much diversity, but one thing was the same everywhere I looked: no jobs.

My feet were blistered by the time I staggered back to the landlady's spare room, and I only had seventy dollars left, having spent ten dollars on food to get me through the day.

"I got a call about the room," she said, as I came in. "I'll be showing it off tomorrow."

"I understand," I said, biting back my fear. I was afraid of the future, but it was strange, because I'd been afraid of the future for months before I'd run away and this was a different kind of fear. There was an excitement hidden in it, and a stubbornness. I was not going back.

I fell sleep instantly when I got to my room, and when I woke everything was dark, there were crickets chirping, and suddenly I didn't feel afraid anymore. I felt ready for the world—even for television—and I decided it was time to learn more about the sin of every day.

After a few minutes I figured out how to turn the television on, and that's when I saw the ad for this show: "Seeking young men and women, age eighteen to twenty-eight, for a new kind of reality TV."

I got on the bus to California the next day.

I just came here to say, I don't know much about reality, but I'm ready to learn and I need a job. I hope you'll consider me for your television show.

November 2011

Character: Someone with a quirky phobia

Action: Affixing reflectors

Setting: Next to a broken-down car

Phrase: "I'm torn"

Cans

Elissa Nelson

"Eating food out of cans is dangerous," the woman tells him. "I see you've got your cans there. Six of them. That's not good."

"I've got my beans, my fruits, three kinds of veggies, and that potted meat I love so much. No carbs—it's a well-balanced meal, isn't it?"

"Fruit cocktail?"

"I like the fruit cocktail the best. You get 'em all, you don't have to pick. Maraschino cherries too. Good stuff."

"That dye—it's toxic."

"Toxic. You drive that car around. That's toxic."

"True, true."

"Course I'd drive a car too—I'm not too good for that, only mine's broken down. There it is right there." He points. "So I can still sleep in it, but she doesn't really go places these days. Unless you push her. I'm not much for that. I just leave her be."

"I see you have reflectors on her."

"That was Pearl did that. She scavenges all that kind of stuff, came over one day for dinner—

black beans, peaches in heavy syrup, creamed corn, these fancy red peppers, and those little onions? And I had some Spam, but she didn't want any. So she came over for dinner and brought the reflectors along. Susie—that's the car—Susie had just broken down and a couple guys helped me haul her off to the side there, but Pearl said it'd be better if people could see her, if she reflected light when people drove by. So now she does."

They're quiet for a moment. The guy eats, the woman stands there, not sure what she's doing. At least that's what it looks like to the guy. He finally asks her: "What're you thinking?"

"I'm torn," she says.

That's all she says. He waits for her to say more, but she doesn't.

"Torn about what?" he asks finally. He doesn't really care—if she's not going to eat, he'd just as soon that she gets out of there and lets him eat. Eat and have his evening. Sit by the fire, smoke his pipe. It's old-fashioned, but he still doesn't like to smoke around a lady. And she's a lady. At first he thought she was one of those social worker types, or just a do-gooder—she's got the nice clothes on, her hair done, no clipboard but she might've left it in her car, a late-model Mercedes, not one of the real fancy ones but it's still a Mercedes.

"I guess I might as well just tell you," she says finally, about ten minutes later. Maybe not really ten minutes, but it's a while.

"Tell me what?" he says, when she doesn't tell him.

"It's about Ed."

"I don't care anything about Ed. What do you know about Ed? What's he got to do with you?"

"I'm his—he's my brother-in-law."

"He married your sister? Must be, because you couldn't've married his brother. He hasn't got one, far as I know. If he did, he'd be lots younger, because he never did as long as I knew Sally Jane."

"He married my sister. Married Lydia three years ago."

"Three years? Has it been that long?"

"Says he hasn't seen you in ten years."

"Nah, he's lying about that. Ten years. Last time I saw him was—shit, ninety-eight, it must've been, and what's this, twenty eleven. Okay. That's fourteen years. Goddamn. Pardon my language."

He's really on his best behavior.

He's not what she was expecting at all, either. Okay, he lives in his car and he eats out of cans he cooks on an open fire. But he's so nice to her.

"What did Ed tell you about me?"

She shrugs.

"Told ya I was a crotchety old asshole, didn't he?"

She shrugs again.

"I am. There's other bits to me, but I am a crotchety old asshole. I was a hell of a dad to him, that's for sure. How's Sally Jane?"

She shrugs again. She sure isn't about to tell this guy what she thinks of Sally Jane, who now regularly comes to all family gatherings, not having any family except Ed.

"How's your sister since she married him? Changed much?"

She wasn't expecting that question either. What was she expecting? She thought either she wouldn't find him here, or he'd be here and drunk, maybe passed out. He might be drunk now, but he's coherent. Cogent, even. A decent guy. She likes Ed—she's liked his stories about his drunk of a dad. Is that wrong to say she's liked them? She has. He wants people to like his stories. And there's a lot of affection in the way he talks about his dad.

He hasn't sneezed yet, though. The way Ed tells it, his dad is all about the sneezes. That must be why he hasn't chased her away yet, though—she doesn't make him sneeze. That was a sad story Ed told about his dad. "I went to visit him once, this was a while back, and showed up with a bag of food for him. Cans mostly. I know what he likes. He took it. And we were sitting by his fire. Then he starts sneezing. And he says, 'Sorry, son, got these allergies. Allergic to people. Different amounts of being allergic—I can put up with about as much of Pearl as I ever could, and the sneezing's just a good excuse to get her out of here—but man, went to the grocery store last week, waiting in line to cash in my cans, and the lady behind me was wearing some kind of hippie perfume. I started sneezing so hard, I had to get out of there and go back the next day.'" She remembers that she and Ed and Lydia sat around for a while guessing what the hippie perfume was. Sandlewood? Patchouli? One of those oil blends you buy at the co-op that's called, like, Peaceful Mist? But she also remembers Ed saying that was the last time he saw his dad. They had a good conversation for a while, then he started sneezing "all hard and dramatic," Ed said, "and I just never went back. Only so much of that a guy can take. Bad enough he was a drunk and a bum but allergic to me? Fuck it." And Ed didn't talk that way.

"Guess I'm not allergic to you," he says to her.

She tries to look like she doesn't know what he's talking about.

"Ed told you anything about me, he must've told you I'm allergic to people."

She's still sort of trying to look like she doesn't know what he's talking about, but she also knows it's no good. She shrugs and nods, like maybe Ed's mentioned it, but he hasn't said much, hasn't told the whole story. Which he hasn't. He doesn't know the whole story. Doesn't know the past thirteen years' worth.

It's like he can read her mind. "It's just gotten worse and worse since Ed stopped coming around. Gotten so mostly Pearl's the only one I can be around at all. Gotta be careful going to the store...bought one of those masks to cover my nose and mouth, it was just getting to where I kept having to run away in the middle of an errand or whatever."

She's still standing there.

"Want to sit down?" he offers. "We could make some coffee—or you want some hot cocoa?

I got some of that mix in the trunk—it's the really good kind. Don't got milk, though it'd probably keep, it's cold enough."

"Tea?" she asks.

"Only kind I like is peppermint," he says, a little sheepishly. "But yeah, you want peppermint?"

"Perfect," she says, and it is.

So she sits down next to the fire with him.

December 2011

In June 2011, Néna Rawdah, proprietress of St. Johns Booksellers and Sledgehammer sponsor since its inception, invited us to have a special contest at her store's anniversary party. We were thrilled to do so, and the event became a monthly series lasting through August 2012. "Eggnog Enchantment," "Jesus Comes Around," "Dog Arms," "The Lake," and "Underworld" come from the St. Johns Booksellers series, judged by Néna Rawdah.

Character: The baby Jesus
Action: Pitching a tent
Setting: The enchanted forest
Prop: A quart of store-brand eggnog

Eggnog Enchantment

Pat Jewett

My favorite eggnog is at Safeway—that's where I'm going now. 'Tis the season for eggnog. It's my favorite time of the year.

The eggnog is lined up next to the milk in the milk section in the cooler. I like the feel of the carton; it is cool to touch, and the carton is smooth.

It's cold and foggy outside, but the eggnog is safe inside the bag inside my backpack. I take a step, and my foot slips a bit on the frozen ground. I'm headed across the St. Johns Bridge and into Forest Park for the night. The bridge looks down into the Willamette River. People sometimes jump from the bridge into the murky river. I think maybe they see the baby Jesus down there.

I pull the collar tighter around my neck. It is very cold up here. There are semitrucks and cars speeding across the bridge, and it is windy tonight. The moon is full, and I like to look at the moon through the cathedral towers on the bridge. Forest Park is there in the haze, and from this end of the bridge it looks enchanted. It is enchanted. Very few people know that. Most people come to hike the eighty-plus miles of trails, but they don't see how the forest is enchanted. I know it is.

Halfway across the bridge, there are flowers along the rail. I am always respectful of the flowers. Someone has jumped and taken their story with them to the baby Jesus in the water.

I hit the traffic button for the walk signal. The entries into Forest Park are numerous, but I like the stairs. Hiking books call the stairs the Ridge Trail Stairs. To me they are just stairs that go up into the enchanted forest.

I adjust my pack by lifting my shoulders up. I can feel the tent pushing against my sleeping bag into the small of my back. That's the problem with just having one compartment in a backpack. Soon I'll find a place to camp and be able to sit on a log and warm my hands over a small illegal campfire.

Most people come up into the park and stay on the main trails. I don't blame them. It is safer on the trails. Most people don't realize how many of us live in Forest Park. If you ever are hiking and feel like you are being watched, you probably are.

There are people who live in the park, and during the day if they don't go into town, they will climb a tree and hide up there during the daytime.

I haven't been here for a while. I had been living in St. Johns and was working part-time at the gas station on Fessenden but it didn't work out. Too many people, too much noise, and someone telling me what to do. I preferred the forest with its quiet enchantment.

I step off the main trail and follow a slight path probably made by a raccoon. I try not to damage the undergrowth as I walk my way farther off the main trail. I am slightly downhill, but there is a place that is level and not readily seen by the nearest trail. For tonight it will be good enough. Tomorrow I will go deeper into the forest.

The moon is still shining through the trees, but I still need my flashlight. I set my pack on the ground and pull out my tent and poles and sleeping bag and the eggnog. I open the carton and take a small swig of eggnog. It is cold and thick as I swallow it.

The poles are the kind that snap into each other and then I have to weave them through the tent holes. I bought the tent on Craigslist last year. It is a Mountaineer two-person tent that I only paid a hundred dollars for. I had to save for it.

With a rock I pound the stakes into the ground and I unzip the tent and throw my backpack and sleeping bag inside.

I clear the ground in a small circle and start breaking off small twigs and find small branches on the ground. Some of them are damp, but I have some dry twigs in my backpack.

I have some newspaper that makes good tinder, and I pile my sticks in a teepee around and over the timber. I reach into my pocket and pull out the lighter I found this afternoon.

The tinder lights, and the campfire lights up the surrounding trees. I lean against the trunk and take another drink of eggnog. If I sit here quietly, the little people will come out of their hiding places and join me in the campfire. Forest Park is home to many things that are unseen by the traveler who just hikes across the trails. I've seen people who walk on all fours, deer, elk, even a bear, dead bodies, even baby Jesus. I drink the eggnog and wait in the enchanted forest.

January 2012

Character: A cake decorator
Action: Washing feet
Setting: A childcare center
Prop: Strong scented candle

Jesus Comes Around

Lisa Galloway

The gift smelled like cinnamon buns, so to un-wrap a Yankee Candle was not a surprise. My family is from the Midwest, if I haven't mentioned it. I rewrapped the candle and brought it home to my housemate, telling her it was from my parents for her. They did not buy her a present in actuality, but I felt bad, because she'd spent Christmas alone.

Well, not completely alone—she'd decorated gingerbread houses with brats at KinderCare and after got so wasted that she burnt her Stouffer's lasagna in the oven. At least watching kids quells her need to make her own babies. Her boyfriend was with his brother's family. She was not invited. She says it is because they are not married, but I doubt they know about her.

I should mention that he wears a two-inch-by-four-inch crucifix around his fat tattooed neck, and he hates me because I'm queer. Queer like short hair and all my friends are gluten-free vegetarians that change their names. He's never said as much, but I gather by his tacky, Catholic icons. Not just the necklace but the god-awful tattoos. That and he never speaks to me. In fact, he stops talking when I enter the room or the door.

Her job before KinderCare was as a cake decorator, but she was too high most days to keep the iced piping even and straight. She smokes a lot more pot now that Jesus comes around. I'm not kidding. His name really is Jesus. Oh and in case you hadn't guessed, he needs a green card. Well, yes, a medical marijuana card would probably help too, but I mean he's not legal.

She loved the candle. I knew she would. She desperately wants to be suburban, live in one of those half tan-siding, half tan-brick, two-car-garage houses. Jesus is the first boyfriend that she's had since high school. She's thirty-two. After she unwrapped the candle, he picked up the glass jar with his fat kid-like fingers and took a big whiff. He smiled at me, lit it, and then nodded.

My housemate and I get along fine, but we have nothing in common except for eating junk food like dehydrated shrimp and pork rinds and watching *Criminal Minds*. I said my friends were vegetarian, but I am not. And yes, my real name is Lisa.

The last fight that I overheard between them was this summer. She'd worn flip-flops all day. I think it was the Fourth of July. They'd been to that abhorrence at the waterfront, and basically her feet were dusty and caked with dirt. He'd told her that she couldn't come to her own god-damned bed without washing them. She was drunk on six-dollar Solo cups of beer, and she wasn't moving. Laziness was one of her hallmark characteristics. So, he ended up washing her feet with a washcloth on the end of the bed. I thought it was tender in a fucked-up way, like he was saving her from herself.

February 2012

Character: A miser

Action: Stumbling up some stairs

Prop: A big, heavy, ornate book

Phrase: "Haters can pound sand!"

Dog Arms

Jack Mahaffy

There was a man who had dogs for arms. There was a dog coming out of his left shoulder, and one from his right. They were both hounds: blood, wolf. Wolf was his right arm. This is how he was born.

It was difficult for the man to do some things, but others came easy. He could hold on to something for a long time. He could never let go of something. The man was rarely cold. As a boy, he unwrapped box after box of vests.

It was hard for the man growing up. But not for the reasons you would think. Here's why. Here's some of the reasons. Please sit. Please stay. Do those two things for a while and quietly so as not to wake the dogs.

There is a whimper, a kind of whimper. Here's what I want you to understand: for most people it is on the inside only. Not for the man. This is a type of whimper that you have probably long since learned by now to keep coiled. But the man's arms bristle. The long lips at the end of each mouth split where your wrist is. Look down. Lie down. Look down to where your hands are. He has wet teeth where your fingers are.

The man loved libraries. Have I mentioned that? I'm sorry. Would you like something to drink? Some tea? Don't mind Blood if she yips— she's just dreaming.

When he was a boy, the man would go to the library after school. The town had two, even though one would have done just fine. It was a small town. The man would go to the first one, the old one, to that one only.

There was trouble in grade school once, in the library once, when he was a boy and the dogs were just pups. The library was old and didn't hide it. There were marble stairs with the sound always and unexpected of different types of heels stumbling up the stairs. There were terminals, sure, and movies in all the modern formats, but the library kept its relics, showcased its older eras. It's okay to be proud of what you are.

The man would go there. He would go into the room with the relics. Have you seen it? It's flanked by two built-in pillars with inscribed pediments— there's a maroon rope strung across the entry with a sign hung where the sag of it is at its deepest. It's a nice place. Tea by itself is suitable, I hope? I have a few cookies, to be honest—hermit cookies—but they were baked for me after my son's funeral. They're delicious and I don't have the recipe. Forgive me if I'm a miser about such things.

So. The library. The room. The boy would crawl under the rope. There was a book there he loved. A big and heavy and ornate book. It could stand his hands. He could hold on to it.

His arms would scamper under the rope. What happened once, when they were pups, was that Blood and Wolf both skittered, growled, pissed on the marble. A boy from school saw him—an older boy. He laughed and pointed at the piss dripping from where your armpits are.

The boy's arms barked. Lunged. The older boy cried out. The boy who would become the man smiled or grunted or was ashamed, probably. He may have thought "I'm sorry" or "Come back" or "Haters can pound sand."

Listen. Thanks for coming. For staying. Will you fetch the kettle for me? It aches to get up anymore these days.

February 2012

Character: A twenty-something dog walker
Action: Backpedaling
Setting: An abandoned hotel on Valentine's Day
Prop: Wrinkle cream

Beast of Burden

Jarrod Schuster

The Long Goodbye had seen better days. Once the pride of honeymooning couples and Valentine's sweethearts, today it was a derelict monument to art-deco excess, and decay.

Chas had been trying to get Henri's dog to commit suicide there for two whole weeks.

Henri, at home grading papers for her "day job" (as she so often felt the need to remind Chas of) had long relegated to him the task of taking Grief for her nightly constitutional. A more aptly named creature, Chas could not imagine. Henri claimed she was named for how she acquired her—an impulse purchase after the "tragic" death of her sister. Chas explained to anyone out of Henri's earshot how she had been named for the misery her presence inflicted.

Grief was some kind of purebred freak of genetic casualty; an inbred, wheezing, bow-legged, smoosh-sinused terror of patchy fur and wrinkled flesh, whose appearance was long announced by nasal snufflings and whine-riddled hacking coughs. Every morning, Grief was subjected to a series of vitamins, pills, drops, and inspections that would make the most cancer-ridden of geriatrics feel relieved at their own plight. And yet, in spite of the genetic minefield the dog straddled, every day Chas awoke to her wheezing hiccoughing need for ablutions.

The Long Goodbye had seemed like the perfect place to finally rid himself of the dog. A warren of exposed, still-sparking wires, tetanus-laced bedsprings, disease-breeding leaky pipes, and a pool long reclaimed by the wet wild. Henri would never forgive him for outright "losing" the dog, but as Grief was born of accident, her demise by such would seem poetic to Henri's literary-attuned mind. "God bless English majors," Chas had initially thought. Now his musings revolved around the capricious cruelty of heavenly beings who plagued him with the thrice-damned burden of "designer" dogs.

Chas stumbled over the half-sealed front doors, hopelessly released Grief as he had a hundred times before, and prayed to half-believed-in deities that tonight the damned dog would finally meet her end. Grief took off, as she always did, investigating the depths of the darkened lobby with a nose that Chas absolutely knew *could not possibly* smell any more than he could.

"I can help your dog, mister."

Chas fell on his own ass in shock, trying to turn the panicked yip he had made in fear into a rough cough. A man in the shabbily mismatched layers of professional street people stepped into the partial light of distant streetlamps, the miraculous buzz and stutter of the still-functional *Hotel* sign above the door lintel.

"Yore dog. I can help 'er," he said again, with the earnest sincerity of the evangelical. Or the insane.

"Ex-hrmm-excuse me?" managed Chas, backpedaling on his bottom away from the ancient stranger.

"I can help yer dog," stated the derelict, "with this!" He flourished a half-used, generic white tube. In black marker, long faded, someone had scribbled *Wrinkel Creem.*

Chas just stared at the man.

Taking the silence as assent, the stranger confidently strode over to Grief, scooped her up in one begloved hand. He unscrewed the cap of the Wrinkel Creem with his stained teeth, liberally squirted out a line of dirty yellow gelatin onto the dog's back. Pocketing the still-uncapped tube, the vagrant began to vigorously scrub the cream into the dog.

Like an unworthy drawing that a child

scrubs at with a fat pink eraser—the dog began to vanish. Tufts of fur, curls of flesh pattered to the floor as the dog, with only a slight snuffle, disappeared.

"T'ain't right to do that to no beast," said the derelict. "What you need is a proper mutt."

As the man shuffled into the empty hotel's depths, Chas realized his dream had come true.

He was so screwed.

March 2012

Character: The bearer of bad news
Action: Selling something
Setting: Neither here nor there
Prop: Boots

Women's Health: Neither Here Nor There

Kathleen Valle

I walked through the café door and the screen door slammed behind me, but customers were not alarmed.

This town was in the middle of neither here nor there, meaning that in any which direction you choose to set off in from this café—there would be no significant destination to reach. They might as well have a sign out front showing each direction:

North 553 Miles to Neither
West 4,492 Miles to Here
East 996 Miles to Land of Nor
South 130 Miles to There

And at each of these places is a dusty old café with people like this—withdrawn and un-alarmed not only by the screen door, but also unresponsive to my boots walking their badass selves down the room. Past the counter, and past the booths of people that looked like they should be sitting in front of a gambling machine rather than across from another person.

I walk toward the back of the room where I see Rodney with his headphones on. He's unable to hear the sound of my boots. I personally don't know how I could live without the sound of these boots. They're the soundtrack to my life. Some women like bangles, some men like keys on their belt loop; I like the sound of my boots. But, that's neither here nor there in this town where people clearly have had too many years of doctor-prescribed meds.

Rodney, now he's a character who always has the soundtrack of his life playing. His hands are always moving to jazz beats when his headphones are on. Rodney always listens to jazz. He sees me approaching, removes his headphones, and sits up all proper-like as if he's been caught off guard or if he's the bearer of bad news.

I sit across from him. His pigmented eyes are more clouded over than I recall. There is an orbiting to his eyes—like jazz records spinning...moving tracks as he scans my presence. It's been a while. His black hands are still now, and I see the aging spots on them. The kind that look like moles or freckles but aren't—it's just a by-product of being old.

"Well," he said, "welcome home."

"Thanks, Rodney. It was 4,492 miles from Here to get here."

"Is that right?" Rodney says, shifting a bit in his seat and looking away from my gaze. He eventually returns his gaze with purpose and asks, "So do you want the good news first or the bad news first?"

I laugh so loud that people actually turn to look.

"Is this some kind of fucking joke? What kind of question is that?"

"I know it's a hard decision. Now, which is it going to be?" Rodney says, hoping to proceed.

I think on it for a bit. Long enough to order coffee—black.

"Bad news first," I say grasping tight onto the mug.

"She's pregnant," Rodney says.

"Okay, and the good news?" I ask.

"She's pregnant," he says.

"Well, there's no good news and there's no bad news—it's just news, Rodney. This is the land of neither here nor there, remember?"

The screen door slams. In comes the Prescription Sales Team ready for their afternoon pitch. A doctor in a lab coat tells how these meds will help this, that, and the other. The doctor's assistant, like an announcer at a horse race, rattles off as quickly as possible the many side effects. The people in the café instantly take out their pocketbooks to pay for medications.

The exchanges are going on, and I ask Rodney if the abortion pill has made its way here yet.

"Oh, that? Man, where you've been. You been gone a long time, ain't you?" Rodney laughs. "Didn't you hear that they give those out free now? These here doctors don't even sell those. Can't even find 'em on the black market no more."

"What do you mean, free?" I ask.

"Well, they's made up them minds to not give no more health care to the womens. So, instead, they give out the abortion pill. It's cheaper than takin' care of the womens, they say."

"So, she has a pill then already, if she wants?" I inquire.

"Yes, she do," Rodney says.

April 2012

Character: A procrastinator
Action: Surprising
Setting: A board-game competition
Phrase: "Batten down the hatches"

The Proposal

Miriam Lambert

Henry was going to propose to Clara on the fifteenth of May, 2009. Her birthday. He'd planned it out down to the shoes he would wear when he took her to Iorio Ristorante: blue, with patent-leather soles that he imagined made him look like a dancer.

But then a week before the day, one of his patent leathers got a hole, and while he was going to have it repaired, the shop he liked best had closed the month before, and by the time he found another one, it was the fourteenth, and they'd only do a rush job if he paid an extra eighty-five dollars up front with no guarantee of workmanship, and Henry's momma hadn't raised no fools, so he left the shop with his patent leathers in his hand, a hole in the sole, and his thin chest swelled with righteous indignation.

By the time he got home, his chest had deflated and he was sunk in uncertainty. He could wear his oxfords. They were old, though, and brown, and he harbored a sneaking suspicion that they made him look as if he were wearing orthopedic supports.

Clara was already seven years his junior. He couldn't propose to her wearing orthopedics.

He pulled the lid off a can of SpagettiOs and dumped the contents into a pot. Stirring the red mass, he turned the problem over in his mind. He could wear sandals. Sandals might be hip. He'd seen a guy Clara's age wearing sandals, and he'd looked hip. But he wasn't sure Iorio Ristorante would let him in wearing sandals.

Then his head shot up—the restaurant! He'd forgotten to make the reservation at the restaurant! Leaving the SpagettiOs on the stove, he hurried to dig his phone out of his bag. When he finally found it, its battery was dead.

Henry sank into a chair. It was a sign, he decided. First his shoes, then the restaurant, now his phone. He was not meant to propose to Clara tomorrow. It was too soon, anyway. They'd only been dating for eight months. He'd give it some time.

Three years later, Henry was determined. This time he'd do it. For certain. The last two years had been bad luck—Clara had gotten a spring flu in 2010, and Henry's weak immune system meant he had to avoid germs. For two weeks they played Battleship over the phone— Henry had called, "Batten down the hatches!"

the first time Clara hit one of his ships, which made her laugh, so he'd kept saying it every time afterward. She didn't laugh at it anymore, but if he stopped he'd feel dumb that he hadn't stopped earlier, so he kept saying it.

In 2011 Henry had had to attend a medical billing conference—bill con, they called it. It was at Disney World, but Clara hadn't gone with him.

But this was the year. Powell's Books was hosting a World Battleship Competition, and Henry had gotten a place for himself and Clara. He put on his blue patent leather shoes and tied the laces with determination. Nothing could go wrong.

People were milling outside the bookstore when they arrived. Most of them were rather young, Henry noticed—in fact, there were a lot of kids about. Some of them were wearing naval commander hats. Doubt niggled at him.

Clara was waiting in the lobby. An inch taller than Henry, she was auburn, slim, and she was wearing a cotton dress and sandals. Henry felt a pang. Maybe he should have gone with sandals after all.

But when he smiled at her, she gave him a small smile in return, and she let him take her hand. They found a place at one of the tables in the back of the room.

As they sat down, Henry cleared his throat. "Clara, I wanted to ask you something."

She raised her eyebrows. Henry swallowed.

"Ladies and gentlemen, boys and girls!" the MC announced. "Please arrange your pieces. You have five minutes."

"Let the World Battleship Championship begin!"

Clara scored the first hit. Henry felt a giggle rising in his throat. He choked. Clara looked at him in alarm, but he couldn't stop himself. He tried to stop the words, but they were coming, and Clara knew it. She reached a hand toward him, but Henry was already on his feet.

"Batten down the hatches! Clara Williams, will you marry me?"

Everything stopped. Everyone was looking at him. Someone tittered. Clara was staring at her board. She didn't meet his eyes.

Heat was rising in Henry's face. He stood there, feeling foolish, feeling stupid, wishing he could sit down, wishing he'd worn the sandals.

He took a step, and then another. He slid across the floor on his patent leather soles.

He spun, and twirled, and hit a board that was sitting at the edge of a competitor's table. The plastic pieces hit the floor and scattered.

Then he was out the door, dancing into the spring air, and Clara was running after him.

"Henry, wait!" she said. But Henry couldn't stop. He was done waiting.

"Catch me," he called, and kept going.

April 2012

In April 2012, Literary Arts requested to host a Mini Sledgehammer contest in honor of that year's Oregon Book Awards, the winner of which would take home a complete set of twenty-five years' worth of Oregon Book Award winners. We jumped at the opportunity, and in the spirit of the awards, we crafted all the prompts to reflect titles of that year's finalists.

Character: Calvin Coconut
Action: Putting makeup on dead people
Setting: The hut beneath the pine
Phrase: "You don't love this man"

The Quiet Man of Wholesome

Jennifer A. Gritt

Calvin Coconut avoided the company of people. His whole goal in life was to be left alone, to live life like a hermit, embrace the silence of the world. Growing up in the small village of Wholesome, Calvin had learned from a young age to avoid the conversations of others. He stood quietly on the edges, offering nothing. The villagers took pity on him, for they thought he was slow of mind. They treated him like an old dog entering his last weeks of life. He moved in and around the people of the village like a mist. Sometimes, upon suddenly noticing him standing there, a villager would startle as if seeing an unexpected ghost. Then she would smile sympathetically and sometimes pat him on the head. It was only the women who seemed to notice him, and he didn't mind the touch. For he knew they just did that as a way to acknowledge him and quickly move on.

When Calvin got older and older, his parents seemed to age twice as fast. His mother and father treated him as the rest of the village treated him—

sometimes even forgetting he was there altogether. On his nineteenth birthday, they died together in their sleep. Calvin felt a wave of sadness when he discovered their bodies—slumbering now for eternity. He would miss them.

When Max the undertaker arrived to take care of the funeral arrangements, Calvin refused to leave his side. Max carefully prepared the bodies for the funeral in silence while Calvin stood in the corner watching his every move. They said nothing to each other—not then, not after. And it was better that way.

Soon after his parents' funeral, Calvin moved a few miles outside of the village. There was an old shack just on the edge of a forest under a giant tree. There, Calvin made his home. Every now and then, a woman in the village would remember Calvin and ask after him. "I think he lives in the hut beneath the pine," someone would respond. "You know, that old hunting shack a few miles south of the village."

For years, Calvin was neither seen nor heard from. Only Max the undertaker seemed to remember him at all. One day, Max ventured out to Calvin's hut. He was retiring, you see, and was looking to pass off his business to a worthy man. Being an undertaker was more than just putting makeup on dead people. There was a ceremony to it, an affection, a love. Only the true of heart could perform this task.

Calvin was working in his garden when Max arrived. The two men did not say a word to each other. Silently, Calvin went in to grab his coat and his hat and locked the door behind him. They walked back to the village in silence.

When they arrived, the butcher's wife ran up to Max. She was crying and waling, for her husband had suddenly died while he was working in his shop. A heart attack. The village was devastated. The butcher and his family were well liked. When the villagers saw that Max had brought Calvin back to the village, they started to wonder why the old man had done this. When they realized that Max was going to have Calvin prepare the butcher for burial, they were concerned and somewhat outraged.

"How can Max do this?" they cried. Some of them secretly wanted to go up to Calvin and beg him to leave the butcher's body alone. "You don't love this man," they wanted to say to him. "You don't love any man."

But Calvin soon put the villagers' fears to rest. For when the butcher was placed in his coffin, he was the image of beauty and peace.

The villagers were amazed that Calvin could prepare the dead for eternity with as much grace as he did. And they were grateful that he was once again part of the village.

June 2012

Setting: The first day of summer vacation

Prop: A road-killed skunk

Action: Spilling coffee

Phrase: "Don't tread on me"

The Lake

Elisabeth Flaum

Jim floored it.

"You can slow down, you know. They won't catch us."

He hit a bump, and my coffee went all over the floor. I swore loudly, and he let up a bit.

"Sorry," he mumbled. "I just don't want to get stuck in vacation traffic."

"Well then take the last day off," I said, sopping up coffee with the assorted paper napkins accumulating in the backseat. "Or wait a week. You don't have to be in such a hurry."

We drove on in silence for several miles. Then the car began to sputter. Jim leaned forward and peered down at the dash. It was his turn to swear as he thumped his fist against the display.

"Damn it! I forgot to get gas."

"And you never got the gauge fixed," I sighed. The car coughed and sputtered some more, and drifted slowly to a stop. Jim leaned his head on the steering wheel. The smell of coffee rose up from the carpet.

"What do you want to do?" I asked. He didn't answer, just kept staring at the gas gauge as if he could fill the tank and start the car by sheer force of will.

"Sweetheart," I said gently, "why don't we try something different?"

"Like what?"

"Look where we are."

He raised his head and looked around. We'd made it just past the boundary into the state park, and immense trees towered over us. Sunlight filtered gently through the leaves. I opened my door; the only sound was a soft breeze just stirring the distant branches.

"Come on," I said. "Let's take a hike into the woods. We can let the horde of summer vacationers pass and pitch our tent right here. Tomorrow we'll find a ranger or someone who can help us with the car."

Jim gazed upward, dappled sunlight falling on his weary face. Slowly he smiled.

"Who needs the lakefront?"

"That's the spirit!" I jumped out of the car, pulling open the trunk. "Water, bug spray, first-aid kit. That's all we need."

Just then the leading edge of the horde of summer vacationers began to pass. RVs, station wagons, and SUVs stuffed to the roof—the entire population of our small college town seemed to be sweeping past. The smell of exhaust and freshly pressed skunk drifted over us. The first wave passed; Jim peered at the small squashed animal lying in the middle of the road. The stink was overwhelming.

"Don't tread on me," Jim muttered. He turned to me with a grin. "Let's get out of here."

Together we pressed through the dense wood. Every once in a while, the sound of passing traffic or the smell of skunk would waft by, soon to vanish in the sounds and smells of the forest. A small brook babbled cheerily nearby. Birds sang. Waving ferns brushed against our jeans. The stresses of the school year fell away; our steps grew lighter and lighter.

The light grew lighter as well. Jim moved ahead of me through the trees. The branches thinned overhead; the babbling of the stream became a soft rushing noise. Jim stopped at what looked like the edge of the world. I hurried to catch up.

"Wow," I breathed. Rather than ending, the world opened up before us. A narrow greensward dotted with wildflowers stretched out, leading to the sandy shore of a sparkling lake. The sun, setting behind us, shone in every color on the crystal-clear water.

Jim took my hand. "Look, our own private lakefront."

I gazed in awe. "How did we not know this was here?"

He shrugged. "Nature's little secret. Our reward for a job well done. Maybe it's a mirage." He dropped my hand and whipped off his sweaty T-shirt. "Let's find out, shall we?"

Suddenly I felt every speck of sweat and dust on my skin, every ounce of dirt that had settled on me over the term, every petty complaint and problem and annoyance of the last nine months, itching all over. I grinned at him.

"Let's."

In moments we'd shed our clothes and, hand-in-hand, dashed madly for the sparkling water, toward the first great plunge of summer.

August 2012

Character: A man waking from an alcohol-
    induced slumber
Action: Shaking hand as though to shake some-
    thing disgusting off
Setting: The underworld
Prop: A book losing its pages

Underworld

Elisabeth Flaum

Jim lifted his head and dropped it again. It went splash.

Groaning, he lifted it out of the puddle. It seemed to weigh far too much; his neck strained from the effort, water running down his cheeks, until he finally rolled onto his back and lay in the wet.

"Never again," he mumbled.

"Heard that one before," said a voice. Jim turned his leaden head till his eyes fell on the familiar shape of Toby lying beside him in the muck.

"How'd we get here?" Jim asked his friend.

"Tequila," Toby answered decisively, crawling to his knees. "Had to be the tequila."

Slowly the men got to their feet, shaking the thick black water from their hands and clothes. Jim rubbed his face, flung a blob of mud from his fingers, and looked carefully around.

"This ain't the Strand, Toby," he said.

"Nope," his friend answered. They stood gazing back and forth. It was a street, or seemed to be; light from invisible streetlamps reflecting in black puddles, a dark musty smell settling over them. Above, there was only blackness, thick and empty.

Jim shivered, claustrophobic.

"The hell are we?" he muttered.

Toby pulled a tattered book from his pocket and flipped it open, pages scattering and fluttering to the ground. He peered intently at the pages in his hands.

"I think we're off the map."

Jim stared down at the sheet floating in the dark puddle at his feet. It glowed gently, like a sickly moon, dimming slowly as it sank into the blackness. He looked up for the source of the light, but found none.

Toby flipped a few more pages, and another leaf took flight. He ignored it, shoving the book back into his pocket.

"Well," he said. Jim looked up expectantly, but Toby had no more to say.

"What do we do now?" Jim asked, his voice nearly a whine.

Toby shrugged. "Dunno. Should be light soon. Then we'll see." He stretched hugely, then looked around for a dry curb or spot of pavement. There was none; he sat back down in the wet.

"Toby, I don't think it's getting light."

Toby snorted. "Don't it always get light? One way or the other?"

"Not this time," Jim whimpered. "We've gone beyond this time—we ain't ever gonna wake up outta this." He glanced at his friend, wringing his hands anxiously, but Toby lay back in a puddle, arms folded behind his head, snoring gently.

"Some pal you are," Jim muttered, lowering himself to the ground. He sat back hard, his hand sinking wrist deep in the muck behind him. He pulled it free and shook it clean, wiping it ineffectively on his jeans.

"C'mon, Toby," he whimpered. "We gotta get outta here, man."

Toby only snored.

Jim huddled shivering beside his friend, every nightmare horror passing through his mind. Ghosts wailed in the distance, the faceless dead lumbered by, sloshing through the thick puddles. Rats chittered and scampered in dark corners. Jim hugged his knees, trembling.

Somehow he dozed.

"Wakey wakey, old buddy!"

Jim peeled open one sticky eyelid. The flesh-toned blur before him resolved into Toby's face. Jim mumbled incomprehensibly.

"Tha's right," said Toby with a deep chuckle. "It's light out."

Jim looked around. The hard ground was as black, the sky overhead as impenetrable as before.

"No it ain't," he cried. "It's no lighter than it was before."

Toby laughed again. "No?" He reached up overhead, stretching his full height, his hands vanishing into the blackness. There was a mighty scraping, screeching noise; Jim clapped his hands over his ears just as a blinding light came pouring in from overhead. The screeching stopped; Jim moved his hands from ears to eyes, peering cautiously through his fingers. A perfect circle of clear blue sky shone down above their heads.

"You remember where we had that tequila last night?"

Jim shook his head, still hiding behind his hands.

"Underworld," Toby said with a laugh. "You got to remember not to use the back door."

Slowly, memory dawned. Jim lowered his hands to his lap and broke out in a broad grin.

"We took the drunk's exit."

Toby shrugged. "Seems appropriate."

Jim clambered to his feet and thumped his friend on the back. "That's great! We're not dead!"

"Not so far," Toby chuckled.

They stared up at the circle of light.

"So..." Jim began.

"You readin' my mind?" said Toby.

"Hair of the Dog?"

Toby clapped him on the back with a reverberant guffaw. "You da man, Jim."

Arm in arm, the two friends sloshed through the muck back into Underworld.

August 2012

In August 2012, Ali Shaw, Sledgehammer's most regular hostess to that point, was offered a once-in-a-lifetime chance to live in Alaska for a year. She decided she couldn't refuse, and she even stayed for two. In the meantime, Mini Sledgehammer contests continued in Portland, hosted by cofounder Kristin Thiel and later by Elissa Nelson and Daniel Granias at Blackbird Wine & Atomic Cheese, though Ali was able to host a few summer contests while visiting from Alaska.

Character: The man with the glint or reflection in his sunglasses
Action: Scabbing over
Setting: A doorway
Prop: Something that has been placed where it should not have been placed

Dream Catcher

Melinda McCamant

Christopher told me he placed the dream catcher in the doorway to snare me if I ever tried to leave. He said this over cinnamon pancakes, and the scent—something like my old blue baby blanket and a sunset—made me think that I was never going anywhere. I dug in, sweet syrup and butter coating my tongue. Oh yes.

Then I found the panties—no, *panties* is too kind. Then I found the crusty thong in the glove box of Christopher's car. They were black and bedazzled, the sort of thong a stripper sheds for her last hurrah.

"Did you find the registration?"

We had been pulled over—sixty miles an hour in a thirty—and Christopher's voice had a hard edge to it. My fingers started to go numb as I held the panties in one hand and the car's registration in my other. I could see my lost expression and the pulsing red and white in the police officer's sunglasses.

"Registration?" It was the cop this time, only his voice seemed kinder than Christopher's—but maybe that was just me seeing me in the mirror lens.

I dropped the panties in Christopher's lap and let the registration fall on top of them.

The cop and I stared at Christopher's lap.

"Those aren't mine," I said, and Christopher chuckled as he handed over the registration.

I was holding it together until he laughed. The car smelled like the stale thong and cowhide. As soon as we were alone, I started to cry. Silly, scratchy, uncontrolled sobs.

Christopher picked the panties out of his lap. "I don't have any idea how those got here." He dropped the thong into the backseat. I looked into the rearview mirror and saw the cop open his door, walking slowly back toward the car. I covered my mouth, tried to quiet down. "You're overreacting," Christopher said and turned his attention to the officer.

I thought of the dream catcher, how it hung a little too far low and how I whacked my head on it every time I left the apartment. I thought of each small knot holding me in place and how I wasn't a dream to be caught but a girl with no dreams beyond sweet syrup and heated leather seats. I felt my tears dry, scab over, fall off my cheeks. And as the officer handed Christopher his ticket, I opened my door and stepped out into the crisp afternoon.

"All right, ma'am?" the cop asked.

The air was cool, but the sun—though low on the horizon—still felt warm on my back and shoulders.

"I'm fine, thank you. I think I'll walk from here."

I looked across the top of the car and once again saw my reflection in the cop's glasses. Only this time my hair was lit up from behind and seemed to glow like a moth escaping a flame. I smiled and the cop smiled back, and I heard the click of the automatic lock as Christopher started his engine and slowly pulled back into traffic.

January 2013

Character: A wispy-haired woman
Action: Tripping
Setting: The library
Phrase: "I walked those streets"

January

Kerrie Farris

The crows crowded in at her feet, squabbling in rough voices over the cold, half-eaten calzone Grace had dropped a moment before. Some of them stood away from the fray, beady eyes trained on her, grumbling and squawking as if their lack of dinner was her fault.

When two birds each grabbed a scrap of crust and flew straight into her face, she abandoned the damp cement bench in front of the library and set off in search of somewhere with fewer feathered ruffians.

Shivering in a gust of wind that nearly took her hat off, Grace skirted a wispy-haired woman in a wheelchair, a wispy-haired palm-sized dog tucked into a fold of the dingy Pendleton jacket draping her hunched shoulders. "I walked those streets, my dear, and there was only half an hour I was ever happy," the woman said to a space well to the left of Grace.

She passed a park, with trees but no grass, where two girls sat on another damp bench, delicately twining each other's hair into spirals, then roughing it up toward the roots with their fingertips. A quick way to turn shiny, soft hair into dreadlocks. Pulling hair in reverse.

Grace left the park behind her. A few silky-feathered crows ahead of her scrattered over, of all things, a pair of ethereal blue panties. Grace lost her footing at the curb, the toe of her boot jutting too boldly into space. She went down, on her hands and knees and chin, onto the damp pavement as the furious crows shredded the panties, strands of soft, shiny elastic breaking as they were pulled the normal way, the harder way, and she wondered if she might not have spent a happier half hour at the library. Even in January, the place was warm.

February 2013

Character: A hostile talking animal
Action: Going to happy hour
Setting: Underneath an underpass
Prop: A child's toy

Cost/Benefit

Daniel Granias

"I told you that wasn't a good idea, Chuck."

"What was I supposed to do? Let them arrest me?"

"You're not worth the handcuffs it'd take."

Chuck sent a heel into the underbelly of Roy, the mange-ridden Labrador, hard enough to throw the hostile hound on his side.

"Shut up, fleabag."

The pair began to gather the damp and torn remnants of clothing and blankets that were strewn in the muddy gutter, wrapping the green camping tarp over the bundle and dragging it out of the rain beneath the convergence of Eisenhower Expressway and the Dan Ryan.

Less than a year ago, Chuck had in fact been worth more than just a pair of handcuffs—millions more. And Chuck hadn't always been Chuck; he was formerly Charles T. Greyson, co-owner of Greyson Motor Industries Unlimited. That was before his brother, Julius, signed the company over to a corporate account that specialized in the electronic digitization of transmissions, a move that left Charles defending a backless, diesel-guzzling freight line, and therefore forced to withdraw all shareholding. This left him with nothing, and his insurance coverage was invalidated after his wife of six years, who provided the plan, revealed her intention to leave Charles for Julius since they'd met at the Golden Nugget happy hour two years ago.

But now Charles was Chuck, and Chuck was on the move.

"I should've left you with Meredith, Roy."

"That bitch? I'd've rather eaten shit."

"You already do."

"Fuck off, you sorry excuse of a bum."

Just as the ragged team slugged their way up to the narrowest part of the ramp, a doll tumbled out of Chuck's tarp. It rolled down the moss-and-mildew-scattered concrete and stuck in a mud bank at the bottom. Its eyes stared up at Chuck in the single yellow glare of the streetlight.

"Why'd you take that from Audrey?"

"She can survive. Her mom can provide her with everything now."

"But why that? She never played with it anyway."

"It was the first thing I bought for her. I doubt she even remembers it."

"She remembers you."

"I'd rather she didn't."

"She's better off."

April 2013

Character: A rich lady

Action: Farting

Setting: The beach

Prop: A song

Forgetting

Pamela Russell Bejerano

I sat on the beach, absolutely engrossed in my book. It was one of those perfect days, rare for the north Oregon coast. The sun was out, the breeze was only mildly distracting, and the number of annoying tourists was minimal. I flipped quickly to the back page, counted the thirty-nine pages left, and continued reading. It wasn't until I finished the last sentence, reread the last paragraph two more times, and slammed the book shut that I realized I was no longer alone.

A woman, at some point, had sat down next to me, her giant beach towel spread carefully on the sand and her equally giant beach bag flopped over by her side. She wore a loose-fitting beach dress that had more colors on it than a sixty-four-count Crayola box. Her thick gray hair was the only thing about her that was neat, tightly pulled back into a ponytail at the base of her neck. Her hat, as wide as her beach towel, rested crooked on her face, half covering her eyes. I wondered that she could see anything, but quickly diverted my attention from her when I realized she was looking at me. The last thing I wanted was to be distracted by this woman, to destroy my beautiful solitude. I buried my face in my bag, desperate to find the other book I had brought with me. I dug and dug, but found nothing. My headphones were a second alternative, and one that would at least give me an excuse to not answer, but I couldn't find those either.

"Damn it," I said, slamming my bag shut.

"Sorry?" she said, jumping at any opening to talk to me.

The euphoria of my wonderful finished book evaporated with the mist floating up off the waves. I was ticked because the last beautiful thought I'd had with that last sentence was gone, now replaced by a woman who chose to sit five feet from me on a beach that started in Washington and ended in California.

"Nothing," I said and wondered whether I should just get up and head back to my car. But damn it, this was my one day, my last day of vacation, and the only dang day I was taking for myself. I decided to chance it and leaned back in my camper chair and let my eyes float out across the waves.

"I am a rich lady," she said, leaning in to be sure I heard her.

I did the airplane leave-me-alone half smile, quick glance out of the corner of my eye, and slight nod, in spite of the fact that her comment had me slightly curious.

"You know that song?"

"No," I said, before I could stop the word from escaping my lips.

She began to sing, humming the notes and lifting and dropping her chin with each note. The tune was completely unrecognizable to me, but I began to watch her in spite of myself.

"Wait," she said, holding a hand in the air and pausing. "I got that last verse wrong."

She started again, smiling and nodding, as if now it was right, though it sounded as random as the first. Suddenly, she stopped.

"Do you know the next verse?" she asked.

She hadn't uttered an actual word, so I didn't know how to answer, so I simply shook my head.

"Sure you do," she said. "It goes like this." She hummed a few more notes, lifting and dropping her shoulders this time along with her chin. "Your turn." Again, I politely refused.

Her eyes narrowed at me, and her face instantly grew sad. I felt my heart sink with the corners of her mouth.

"But you're so young. How could you not know the song?"

Again, I had no idea what she meant, so I said nothing.

"Try," she said, standing and sliding her towel within inches of my chair. When she sat, a loud fart escaped and reverberated on her towel. Her eyes grew wide, then her mouth opened, and she threw her head back and laughed. It was one of those beautiful, full laughs that moves even the bottom of your feet. Falling under her spell, I found myself laughing along with her. When she opened her eyes and saw that I was laughing too, she laughed harder.

"I did that once in the middle of class, during our AP exam." She laughed more, taking several deep breaths before she continued. "The proctors tried not to laugh, but they did. Then so did the two students next to me. Then, you know what?" She raised her hand in the air and landed it on my forearm, leaning in to me as we both giggled even harder. "Then the whole class started to laugh." It took us several minutes to stop laughing and breathe enough to be able to talk.

"That's a great story," I said.

"You know the best part?" She turned and looked at me, her intense blue eyes finding a place in my mind and holding me there. A beautiful smile spread ear to ear, revealing yellowed, tin-filled teeth. "We all passed!"

"Sing with me," she said, and again started humming along.

Giving in to the forgetting of my second book and my headphones, I began to hum along. This only encouraged her, and her song grew louder, encouraging me even more. Soon the two of us were lifting and dropping our shoulders, leaning in to each other, swinging back and forth on our hips, and singing out at the top of our lungs. I couldn't remember the last time I had had this much fun.

"Nena!"

A distant voice called out, and my new friend disappeared as suddenly as she had appeared. Her face was stone and expressionless as her eyes scanned the beach then stopped. I followed her gaze and saw a young man and woman walking quickly toward us.

Before they reached us, she leaned in to me, putting her mouth next to my ear. "Don't let them stop your song, my beautiful one," she whispered. "Ever. Promise?"

I turned and looked at her, but her eyes had not left the man and woman. "Promise?" she said again, this time with more emphasis.

I took her hand in mine and turned her head so her eyes refocused on me. "I promise."

Briefly, a smile reappeared on her face.

"Nena!" the man said. To me he said, "I'm so sorry," then turned back to her before I could reply. "Nena, you know you are not supposed to leave the home. How did you get out this time, huh? They said you were locked in your room and couldn't get out."

"She was no problem, really," I tried to interject, but my voice was drowned out by their ridicule of her. When I realized they had packed her towel and were about to shuffle her away from me, I stood and yelled.

"Hey!" It worked. All three stopped and turned to look at me. I had no idea what to say next and stood awkwardly for several moments. "We...we weren't done with our song," I finally stuttered.

Nena smiled. "I am a rich woman," she said. "Do you know that song?"

I looked from the man to the woman, whose annoyance was obvious by their pursed lips and one-eyed raised brow.

I looked back to Nena. "Don't you mean 'I am a rich lady'?" I asked.

Her face went blank.

"She has Alzheimer's," the woman said. "She'll forget you before she's back in her room."

July 2013

Character: A gardener

Action: Recycling

Setting: A thrift store

Phrase: "The mountain is out"

Bottling

Peter D'Auria

This thrift store is different. And yet there is no sign indicating this. It stocks a wide variety of vintage clothes, obsolete electronics, and out-of-print books. Yet there is no sales staff to inform you of this. Because, despite this very respectable inventory (Leonard and I once found a near mint-condition copy of *Bat Out of Hell* with not a scratch on it, which we still listen to about twice a week), this thrift shop specializes in a different sort of used product: Used-Tos.

Yes, once a month the thrift shop will hang a faded flag with a picture of Mount Fuji outside its window—"The mountain is out," Leonard will say over the phone—and we will sprint down to the shop. There is a room in the back filled with Used-Tos, each one labeled and bottled carefully: *Used-to-date. Used-to-go-to-the-zoo. Used-to-live-across-the-street.*

"I wonder how they get them into bottles," Leonard says, and I tell him I don't know. When we ask the owner how he gets them, he just gets angry. "They are Used-Tos," he says. "People do not use them anymore. Why shouldn't I have

them? Are you going to buy something or what?"
And we do, we buy as many bottles as we can,
and then we go sit in Leonard's garden and drink
them. It is, Leonard remarks, a kind of recycling.

Sometimes they are sad. Last month I drank
a particularly poignant *Used-to-love-me* and I
couldn't get out of bed for two days. Sometimes
they're beautiful. *Used-to-go-to-the-beach*es are
always wonderful. They have a glow about them.
Sometimes they're just weird. Yesterday the flag
was out, and that afternoon, as we sat under his
pear tree, Leonard looked up after his first sip
from a bottle and said, "This is one of mine." I
asked him what it was. "It's about my mom," he
said. "When I was little she used to take me
down to her garden. I used to help her pick
string beans and pull weeds and stuff."
Leonard's mother had passed away just last year.
"Can I have a taste?" I asked him, and he shook
his head and said, "I don't think so."

I went back to my *Used-to-have-this-cat*
and Leonard finished the bottle. We sat for a
minute and then Leonard went inside. I looked
around at Leonard's own garden—his tomatoes
in rows, raspberries on strung wire, and the
thought struck me that someday this moment
itself would be labeled and bottled, sitting in a

back room filled with old friends and lovers and dead pets.

December 2013

In early 2013, Elissa Nelson, longtime participant and supporter of Sledgehammer, fell ill. Over the summer, several friends she'd made at Sledgehammer began to meet with her for private Mini Sledgehammer writing sessions, but we saw her less and less at the official events.

In November, the world said goodbye to Elissa, and we at Sledgehammer mourned the passing of a great friend and writer. Ali hosted a Mini Sledgehammer with friends in Alaska featuring prompts that described Elissa:

> Character: Someone terminally ill
> Action: Squinting one eye
> Setting: On the front porch
> Phrase: [Silence]

Though the participants didn't know Elissa personally, they were inspired to write stories in memory of their loved ones. Ali summed up the event with:

While Sledgehammer was founded to help shatter the fiction writer's block, this combination of prompts led us all to write nonfiction. Grief, it turns out, is a topic most people can relate with and most writers can convey.

It was a beautiful moment to hear the true stories as these writers honored someone they'd lost. And it was not a moment to pick a winning story to post on the website. We'll keep our stories to ourselves this time, but we invite you to write your own story with these prompts. And we hope you'll find healing in the process.

Back home in Portland, Daniel Granias, whom Elissa had introduced to Sledgehammer, dedicated this story to Elissa's memory.

For Elissa Nelson

Character: A timekeeper

Action: Penciling it in

Setting: At a calendar sales rack

Phrase: "Time flies like an arrow, fruit flies like a
banana"

Purple Pillows

Daniel Granias

In my dreams, my father rides on the back of a whooping crane. It flies through an amber sunset, its neck undulating in a long *S*. Together they splash and patter in the high tide while the rhino burrows its great iron horn in the glittering sand searching for nematodes. The crane takes my father's belt in its long beak and throws him into the dusty lavender thickets, where he rolls across their dense beds under the cattail reeds that tower eight stories high. The king of the nematodes carries an hourglass with three bulbs: one for red sand, one for yellow, and one for green. When he turns the glass, the sky turns gray, and my father and I are sitting in a doctor's office, waiting for the nematode secretary to call our name.

"Bastille! Bastille! I've been calling you for the past century! Where have you been? You've missed your bicentennial treatment again, now we must pencil you in for the next millennium, and we're booked through Julaugustary!"

The day-by-day calendar on the desk curls its pages into lips that say, "Time flies like an arrow, fruit flies like a banana!"

With a flourish, my father throws on a lime-green doctor's coat and lifts me in its folds. He takes me to the bookshop he owned, to the corner where my mother quilted the pillows and blankets in so many shades of violet, plum, and indigo.

It is there I wake, beneath the cherry-cedar rocking chair where he'd take me in his lap and read me tales of places near and far, while I stared at the pictures of birds and mammals on the calendars we sold on the rack by the register. The pillows still smell and feel like my mother's bosom; it was so long ago, I fit in the linen nest of her apron before her cancer took hold for the year that followed, each day feeling like a month, each visitation hour like a second.

Now I'll sort and stack the pillows, activate the register, and flip the paper clock in the window back and unlock the doors as parents and children visit our rows of pop-ups, pictures, and puppets, and I'll assume my place in the cherry-cedar rocking chair and read the next tale to this afternoon's visitors just as my mother and father did.

January 2014

Character: A reformed omnivore

Action: Choosing bananas

Setting: The bottom of the bowl

Phrase: "Oh yes, I know the Muffin Man"

The Difference Between Snow

J. B. Kish

He reached out, choosing bananas again. He always chose bananas on colder days, when the snow had drifted up against the front of his cabin like the lip of cake frosting. Jerking his massive wooden front door open, he welcomed a sharp, cutting breeze against his cheek and shook it off. Mother winter was kissing him awake. Kisses were always their brightest in the morning. Not like sundown.

Jack Shadowsong stepped out into the high-desert sunlight and carefully peeled one of his bananas from the bottom up. He took an enormous bite, and carefully wedged the rest of his fruit lunch into his parka. The others stuck out from his belly like lumpy tentacles, giving him a queer look. He chewed complacently, staring at the fruit in his pocket. He had a long day ahead of him. Longer now since he'd become a—what did his daughter call him?—*a reformed omnivore*. Seventy-five years of sugars and elk and hamburgers down at the gas station had made him sluggish and slow.

"You're an old buffalo," his daughter Suzy told him. "You'll die in these mountains an old buffalo, Papa. You have to start eating better."

And so, much to his chagrin, Jack Shadowsong had banana lunches and fruit dinners, and fruit breakfast, and fruit, fruit—

"Fruit," Jack muttered. "God, I hate fruit." He spit the rest of his banana, and it disappeared into the snow at his feet. And then he was off, to the bottom of the bowl, to watch the young skiers get in fistfights with snowboarders and drink until they were red in the face.

"That was Justin Jackson's new hit single, 'Oh Yes, I Know the Muffin Man,' and you heard it first, right here on KRSMACK Radio."

The radio DJ's voice blared through the speakers at the base of the ski slope near the ticket booth. The line was down to the parking lot. And the children were already screaming. Jack hadn't even made it into the lodge for coffee yet before his boss was waving him to the chair lift for a quick relief shift. That's what he called them. "Relief shifts."

"The only smoke break that took forty-five minutes," Jack thought to himself. But there he was, standing in line and checking tickets and thinking to himself about the coming night.

Jack could stand for hours at a time. He didn't mind his job. He didn't mind standing, and pressing the button when a child fell down onto its face. He liked picking them up, brushing the snow off their noses and helping them onto the lift. He didn't mind all the money, and the white people, and the radio DJ, or the lack of coffee. What Jack minded was the snow. What Jack minded, was the spirit of the mountains.

"You'll die in these mountains, Papa. An old stubborn buffalo," his daughter told him. And maybe she was right. There was no fruit for stubbornness. And so maybe he would die in these mountains.

"Hell," Jack thought to himself. "Maybe I'll die right here in line, taking tickets and listening to radio DJs. Maybe I'll turn into a Popsicle and they'll put a flashlight in my hand." But he wouldn't leave his mountains. He wouldn't leave mother winter.

What Jack minded was the snow. The white snow. The perfect, white, reclaimed snow that they made in machines so the money would come and the music would play and the snowboarders would fight. Jack hated the snow because he couldn't tell what of it was new and what of it was old. He couldn't tell what mother winter had brought him and what the lawyers made with their documents and their paper and their signatures.

Jack missed the days when he was a boy and he didn't have to think about the people on his mountain. When snow was snow. And winter was winter. And the cold was—

"Hey, asshole, are you paying attention?"

Jack's eyes fluttered to life and landed on the boy holding out his ticket. Jack narrowed his focus, and then his expression fell. He feigned a smile, scanned the ticket, and the boy got on the lift.

When the sun dropped down, and the temperatures reached their lowest, the mountain emptied, and Jack found himself still standing at the bottom of the bowl. Mother winter's kisses were at their darkest, and there was no shaking that kind of cold. Not until he was home and in his bed. But that night, Jack decided to stay a little while longer and stand in line. With no tickets to scan and no little children to help to their feet. Jack stood in the bowl and remembered the time when he was little. When the snow was really snow and there was no reason to think otherwise.

"You'll die in these mountains, Papa," his daughter told him. "An old stubborn buffalo." And maybe she was right. Maybe he would.

June 2014

Character: A bike rider
Action: Receiving a message
Setting: During a summer storm
Prop: A guitar

What Comes Next?

J. B. Kish

"A-sharp. G. Show him, Allison, show him."

Allison, breathless and clothes sticking to her paper-like skin, repeated her mantra, riding the ten-speed up the lonely saguaro-riddled highway with strange determination. The monsoon rain was biting at her neck, the summer storm overtaking her faster than she'd thought something naturally capable. Here she was, a thirty-two-year-old bicyclist from Portland, Oregon, terrified for the first time in her life to be riding a saddle at three in the afternoon.

"A-sharp. G. Show him, Allison," she barked to herself. "Show him you can do this."

She kicked the pedals down, allowing the pendulum of momentum to suck her heels upward; then she repeated this process again and again. Soon, the rain came in horizontal sheets and slapped against the cracked pavement rhythmically. In a matter of seconds, her picturesque view of the Catalina Mountains was swallowed by gray—what was it, clouds? Fog? She focused on the road in front of her—the only three feet she could make out between eyelid-soaked blinks and bursts of air she ejected from her bottom lip in an effort to shake free her face from that unavoidable soaking.

"A-sharp. G."

She plucked at the guitar strings of her mind, suddenly imagining herself in front of the mirror hidden in her childhood home's attic. She was holding her father's guitar in her arms, wondering desperately how to play the song he'd taught her. The one that he played for her when she was afraid to go to sleep at night. Afraid of the monsters of adulthood.

"Think, Allison," she demanded of herself. "What comes after G. Think, goddamn it."

But she couldn't remember. The storm yawned once more, spooking her toward the center of the road. A single pair of headlights approached, blinked, and soared past. She thought to herself how close she might have come to death had she accidentally steered in front of the car just moments before.

"A-sharp. G. Show him you can do this."

She closed her eyes and tried to shake the thundering clamor of storm. She pumped harder and harder. Running from something she wasn't entirely sure of. Running from the message she'd received just five days earlier. Running from those words on the voicemail.

"Goddamn it," she cried, taking a mouthful of rain. "What comes after G?!"

"Straighten your hand, and press here."

She imagined her father, suddenly sitting next to her, holding her hand in his own.

"It's important you learn discipline," he told her, his words that special mixture of warmth and emotionless instruction that only a father can produce. "It's important you learn, Allison. I won't always be here to help you." He looked at her, his expression flat in the attic mirror.

"A-sharp. G. Then what?"

"Show him, Allison."

"A-sharp. G. Then what?"

"Allison, it's your mother. Where are you?"

"Straighten your hand. Then press hard here."

"Allison, I've called you five times. Don't make me do this over voicemail."

"No, press harder here."

"Allison, it's your father. The doctors say he fought so hard..."

"Show him, Allison. Show him you can remember what comes next."

"Allison. It's your father—"

January 2015

By this time, regular host Daniel Granias had begun rotating the hosting and judging duties with Mini Sledge regular J. B. Kish so they could each compete every other month. In addition, each month's winner was invited to be a guest judge the month after winning. January 2015 marked Jeremy Da Rosa's first win, and he enjoyed judging in February so much that he offered to be part of the host rotation as well.

Character: Siri
Action: Exercising
Setting: January 1915
Prop: Salt

Milk Starring Sean Penn

Jeremy Da Rosa

It was the largest glass of milk I had ever seen. I'm no stranger to milk (I've got most varieties memorized), but this was the biggest glass I'd seen. Thirty-two ounces at least. Next to it the sugar shaker on the table looked like a salt shaker.

The waitress brought me a straw, which was kind but unnecessary.

"I'm pretty good with milk," I said.

"Siri," I asked, "what is the Guinness World Record for largest quantity of milk drank in one sitting?"

Siri didn't know. I stood up in the brown diner. There was a belt of square windows strung around its waist and a fence of bushes between the windows and the street. A marathon was breathing heavily by, and I was convicted about my lack of exercise. I returned to my milk.

A search through the bowels of the internet revealed the milk-drinking record was two cows past a full herd: a man named Samuel Scott Walker held the record with 2.5 gallons of whole milk drank in one sitting. The asterisk next to the stat showed a sitting was considered forty-five minutes.

This was beyond me—no matter how much I loved the thick, natural, soy-based alternatives. I needed to train, and to train, I needed to talk to the best.

According to Classmates.com, Samuel Scott Walker was born on January 30, 1915, in Tillamook, Oregon, which made sense—where else would the world's best milk drinker be born other than in the town that produced the nation's best dairy products?

But 1915, that's one hundred years ago! The odds that this proud man still walked among us were thinner than a glass of nonfat.

May 2015

Character: An ice-cream vendor

Action: Recycling

Setting: In the rain

Prop: Smoke

Burnt Ice Cream

Elizabeth Grace Martin

Maven got a rush from the flick of the lighter. The burn of the cigarette down her lungs felt like the appropriate amount of unhealthy. Fuck healthy. She liked smoke and ice cream. She even dyed her hair to add a swirl of gray to damage her streak of brunette.

After being recycled in the foster care system, she fated herself into a runaway. That's when the gray came—a nod to the wisdom she decided she was due—not the wisdom she'd earned.

The smoke came before the streets. Fire was home. Maven didn't much like the term *arsonist*. She preferred *creator*. She burned ugly away. It gave her control over something—at least that's what her therapist claimed. Fuck him.

She didn't see him more than once. Maven didn't see anyone more than once. Judgment stays at bay when you don't let people know you. Only she needed to know her.

So she hopped trains and claimed the title *explorer*. She slept in barns with livestock and thought herself a farmer. She was neither. Maven was a homeless runaway, but a good marketer. But even runaways need a break; even runaways need an identity.

The train Maven was currently riding stopped for fuel or to load or unload. Fuck if she knew. But the day was bright, sweat grouped at the bottom of her spine.

"Ice cream," she said to no one. No one was her favorite audience. The jump from the train car to the red rocks below sent a shock up her legs—the kind that reminds you you're still alive. Pain, fleeting but passionate.

Maven lit her first cigarette of the day and walked along the tracks until the town came into view. She'd never been to Arizona before, but it felt like every other place. She lit another cigarette as soon as she stomped her first one out on the metal track.

The tracks went straight and she curved to the left. The siren song of the ice-cream truck was calling her. It sounded like home.

On the first main street she crossed, she pickpocketed an empty-faced stranger. The siren was getting closer.

"Banana split," Maven called to the ice-cream vendor.

A man with naturally gray hair and a news-boy cap popped his head out of the freezer and into her view.

"Hi there, miss. How are you?"

"Banana split," Maven repeated, ignoring the vendor's inquiry.

"Talkative, aren't you?"

"Not to strangers."

"How do you 'pect to make friends?"

"What?" Her attitude was showing through. This was already the longest conversation Maven had had in months. "Fuck, man, you got a banana split or not?"

"Fresh out. *Fudgsicle?*"

"Whatever."

"It's on the house," he said, eyeing Maven's unwashed hair and wrinkled clothes. "Take care."

She wanted to be snotty. She wanted to ruin him with words. But Maven bit her tongue and accepted the Fudgsicle before it melted under the Arizona sun.

She nodded at him. He smiled, toothy. It was the best he was going to get from a runaway punk, and they both knew it. Maven couldn't shake the interaction. No one was nice to her. She gave no one a reason to be. She felt uneasy about it. She followed the ice-cream vendor that day, touring the city in his shadows.

When the sun dunked into the night, he parked the truck, and Maven kept watching it. She flicked her lighter in front of her. Up and down, the flame teased her, called her like the siren song of ice-cream trucks.

She answered.

The fire started to burn slowly. Deliberately. The tires melted into puddles, and the ice cream would soon do the same. She watched the damage long enough to feel satisfied. The smoke pillowed the sky into more darkness, and she walked away, without remorse, into the rain.

The fire won again.

June 2015

Character: A drummer

Action: Tipping a waiter

Setting: A cemetery

Prop: A cellar door

Whiskey Ginger

J. Turner Masland

I can never tell if the flirtation from a food service worker is because they find me attractive or if they just want a big tip. Either way, I love the attention.

It is June, and I am two weeks into a new city. Feeling lonely and a little lost, my evenings are spent seeking human contact. Anything from eye contact to everlasting friendship. Especially after my arduous days in a sterile and soul-crushing call center, dealing with customer complaints all day, I need a little real-life face-to-face interaction.

All the stools at the bar in the restaurant around the corner from my dingy sublet are fully occupied, so I grab a table. Which I don't mind, but it makes it harder to chat with my fellow patrons.

"Hi. My name is Tony, and I will be taking care of you tonight. What can I get you, handsome?" The waiter looks down over his pad with a twinkle in his eye. I start to sweat. Usually I only get attention from men when I am four or five whiskeys in at the trashy gay bar downtown.

I feel that electric charge that hits the pit of my stomach and zaps my groin that comes with flirting with a really cute guy.

"Whiskey ginger."

"Coming right up."

With each drink comes more eye contact, more sly smiles, a few probing questions. All from him. Again, I can't tell if he wants the tip or he wants...the tip. But I am hungry for his attention. And with each drink, I get bolder. And happier. And warmer.

Soon it's approaching midnight.

"Well, handsome, my shift is over. Can I cash you out?"

"Of course," I reply, "only if I get your number."

"Better yet," he says, "why don't you join me for a walk? I always need to unwind after my shifts. And it's a full moon. Perfect for a late-night stroll."

Fuck. Yes. I smile and nod.

It's one of those magical summer nights. Cool breeze in the air, but the sun's warmth from earlier is radiating off the concrete. The moon is bright, and the stars seem to dance.

We wander through the neighborhood. I tell him about my move and my job, and I stop when

I start to mention my loneliness. He listens and nods.

Soon we hear drumming. Which feels odd. Mostly because we are approaching the Lone Fir Cemetery.

I look to my handsome waiter. "Drumming?" I ask.

"It's June and a full moon in Portland," he says. "I am surprised this is the first drum circle we've stumbled across."

We enter the cemetery. The gravestones seem to glow fluorescent in the moonlight. I expect there is a fire. Most nocturnal drum circles I experienced back east were always around a campfire.

But not this one. A few dozen drummers are around an angelic statue. The marble figure looks up to the sky, as if it is beseeching a higher power. The rhythm is steady. I can't tell if it's been rehearsed or improved. But it's animalistic. Along with the drummers are a few dancers, with dark fabric over their arms, looking like bat wings.

Time is lost. I don't know if we stand there for five minutes or five hundred. That electricity in my stomach is replaced by the beats of the drummers. The dancers turn from bats to angels to birds. They swirl and fly and float. The stars start to spin, and the moon pulses with the rhythm of the drummers.

Through the chaos, I lock eyes with one drummer. A light seems to emanate from him, and his gaze feels inviting. As if he wants me to join his collective. As if I was brought here, to this graveyard, for that purpose. And for a brief moment, I want to.

But then Tony's warm breath is on the back of my neck as he whispers into my ear. I can't hear what he says over the drummer. But feeling my handsome waiter's face so close to my own sends that zap of electricity back through my body, overpowering the rhythm of the drummers.

Tony's hand slips into mine, and he leads me away into the night.

Had I know that I would be found dead, head cracked open and thrown through a cellar door into the basement of an abandoned building, I would have stayed there. At the drum circle. Taking the drummer's invitation and joining the dancers. Using my feet, my hands, my body to contribute to the rhythm. Had I known, I would have never taken that handsome waiter's hand.

December 2015

Character: Nobody

Action: Breaking and entering

Setting: A fireplace

Phrase: "Not as bad as last Christmas"

The Giving

Sarah Farnham

the girl dangled her legs over the bed. her little brother sat in front of her.

'whaddya think this christmas will be like?' she asked.

'worse than last.'

she chewed on the blanket and sighed. she knew he was right.

'what's for dinner?'

'dunno.' he slumped as he sat there, back caving over as he pulled strings out from the carpet.

their mother, dressed in skirts and elegant cardigans, started when they were three. 'your only task in life is to give back,' she would say, smiling. 'it's better to give than to receive.' the only holidays they remember were spent volunteering at the shelter, passing out food for the homeless or the domestic victims of the gritty streets of philadelphia. their father, while still in the picture—he stayed home and watched football. he preferred not to listen to their mother.

they didn't have any extended family. no cousins to play barbies with, no aunts to lecture them, no uncles to tease them. they were no good at making friends, either. two years apart, they much preferred the company of each other. teachers marveled at it, but the other kids sneered. they teased her for hanging with her baby brother, and they tortured him for wanting to hang out with a girl.

but they were the coolest people they knew. everyone else was kinda dumb, and definitely didn't understand the intricacies of their daily life.

they were not cinderella children—it wasn't as if they counted lentils in the fireplace or peeled potatoes for days on end. they did, however, make their beds and wash the dishes. their mother asked them to, and they obliged, gratefully. if a grownup in their life, say at an uncommon party, would ever laugh at them, wondering how children were so well behaved, they would stare blankly, uncaring, until that grownup wandered off. their eyes frequently glazed off in conversations with teachers—they always had the right answers, but there was more than one educator who thought, 'there is something wrong with those two.'

if they knew about it, they had shrugged it off long ago.

because they knew something no ordinary adult knew.

their mother, a kind and benevolent force, had taught them the secret to life.

she taught them to volunteer first. being small children, they thought of nothing but pleasing their mother. they went about, merry, caroling and passing out food and smiling at strangers, a tiny movement unto themselves. after school, they collected bottles for the men who would ride by and collect them late at night. they had an allowance, and it was spent on other people. coats for the cold bridge people, hats for the dirty children who roamed the streets. a can of beans for the woman who always walked by at noon on tuesday.

the girl asked first.

'mother?'

'yes, darling?'

'other children sometimes—'

'what have i told you about other children?'

'that they don't know what i know.'

'which is?'

'that the world is operating on a different level entirely, and that they are wasting their time and money and energy.'

'correct. you were saying?'

'nothing.'

the girl sat on her bed at night, thinking. she knew some things, that was sure. she knew that the world was keeping score; she knew that someone was always watching; she knew that she needed to always do more.

she also knew she was not happy, because it was never enough.

he felt the same. they sat on the swings, bundled up in the cold. december was windy but bearable. they allowed themselves a small break in collecting cans twice a week. he decided to ask her instead of mother. 'sis—why don't other children do what we do? don't they know better?'

she shook her head. 'no, because they are silly. they might have a chance to change, but they're starting so late...'

'what's going to happen to them?'

'i'm not sure; mother never told us that part.'

he chewed on his lip. he whispered, 'do you ever think we should be doing more?'

she turned to him and looked visibly relieved. 'all the time. i just don't think it's enough.'

he sat forward, excited. 'i've been thinking

about something.' she nodded. 'what if we—what if we did what *He* did?'

she frowned. 'that's blasphemy.' she started to swing again.

he scooted forward again, irritated. 'it's not. He wants us to.'

'why do you think that?'

he started to breathe faster. she looked over at him sharply. 'don't trigger an attack.'

he shook his head. 'i won't. just listen.' he got off the swing and stood in front of her.

'He started poor, right?' she nodded. 'He started with nothing, just by giving everything He could. and eventually He built a factory, and an empire, and He was able to *really* give everything.' she nodded again. he folded his arms. 'i think the only way we'll ever truly escape death is if we do the same. He's still alive, right?'

she stopped swinging. 'we could live forever, just like Him. His power is what keeps Him alive, after all. the Giving.'

'exactly. it's just common sense.'

she frowned slightly. 'i know we can always do more. i know we always have more to give. so what are you thinking? what's the big thing?'

he leaned in, his eyes glittering. 'we can do what He did.'

she gasped. 'we—we could—'

he nodded. 'it's not enough that we give what we can. we need to be invisible, like Him. we need to build His empire.'

'what if He sees us?'

'are you serious?' he asked. 'even better.'

'what if we go to the same houses?'

he whispered. 'then we would see Him. maybe compare notes, see what we could do better. sis—we could *see Him*.'

she stood up suddenly. 'i'm in,' she said.

they began preparing that night. they had exactly one month to train. he had started collecting supplies (ropes, backpacks, climbing gear from his dad's abandoned hobby) before he had even told her, but she added the fine details he knew he needed her for. the small headlamps were her idea.

as smaller-than-average children go, they were pretty quiet already. but they practiced themselves to be downright silent. their mother beamed as they walked around the house, doing their chores and storing items like squirrels.

'children,' she said one day. 'i just want to congratulate you. you've been working so hard, and giving so much—but i also want to encourage you to work just a little harder.' she pinched their cheeks, frowning as she noticed the smudges of coal. using a thumb and her tongue, she rubbed at their faces. 'death won't escape itself.' she twirled around the corner in a swirl of skirts and chanel.

the night came. they were ready and executed their task with skill and ease.

and as the police prepared to cart them off, they could hear the buzz of the radio.

'ten-four. on your way?'

'yeap.'

the window was open.

one policeman, standing outside of the car, turned to the other. 'what happened tonight?'

'coupla kids, breaking and entering. left a bunch of useless shit in the living room. fifth house this week.'

'jesus.'

'santa nuts. at least it's not as bad as last year.' the children smiled at each other in the backseat.

January 2016

Character: Cat Stevens

Action: Parallel parking

Setting: The Blue Ridge Mountains

Prop: A two-hundred-dollar travel voucher with
United Airlines

Parallels

Summer Olsson

Trees put the blue in the Blue Ridge Mountains. And it was a tree that put the dent in my dad's blue Chevy Impala too. So many trees in the forest where we live—where I used to live until a couple weeks ago—and they release this gas, like, that the air looks blue, from far off. My dad's '63 Chevy got backed into a tree. By me, a' course.

I'd been trying to take my driver's test twice now, and it was frustratin' my dad more'n me. He was giving me drivin' lessons on the side because as soon as I was legal, he could stop cartin' me and my li'l sisters around so much and get back to playin' his mando in the garage. These lessons stressed us both out and made me cry usually and there was a lot of yellin' 'n' stuff. The thing we were workin' on, when I backed into the big oak along our lane, was parallel parking. That was what I messed up the worst on the last test. The first test we don't talk about. But by now I was pretty good at not screamin' when an animal crossed the road in front of me, or missin' stop signs altogether, or slammin' on the brakes when the light changed to yellow.

Parallel parking, though, was still causing me trouble. My dad kept saying we needed to work on my nineteen-point turn. After I bumped—"Which is what the bumper's for!" I yelled—he stormed into the house and didn't come out again.

Later, in school, my friend Shuggs, who already had his license and drove his dad's pickup on the weekends, said he knew a real good trick for parallel parking. Now this from a guy who thought Allen Ginsberg helped him find a parking space. I don't know where he got that idea, but if we were ever in town, lookin' for a spot close to wherever, and it was real busy and nowhere to park, Shuggs would start goin', "Oh, Allen Ginsberg, we call on you to help us! Oh, Allen Ginsberg, great god of parking spots." I thought he was makin' a joke because we read that guy in English class and he was a hippie poet guy. But you know, most of the time we got a parking spot right away. Anyway, Shuggs said that Cat Stevens was the patron saint of parallel parking. All I needed to do was play his music while I was doin' it, and it would be like magic—I'd just be good at it.

My third time to take the test was comin', and I think Dad was gettin' a little worried about it, because he promised me two hundred dollars if I passed! "I promise," he said. "I'll give you two hundred dollars and you can buy a guitar or a whole bunch of whiskey or whatever the hell you want."

What could it hurt, really? So I got a Cat Stevens tape. I had to go to that place, Charlie's Records and Tapes, which smells like a wet cardboard box, but my dad's Impala only has a tape deck. I got *The Very Best of Cat Stevens*. I went out to the yard the next afternoon, after school, to practice parkin' between two trees. Then the craziest thing happened. Maybe it was because music helped me focus more or somethin', I told Shugg later, so he wouldn't think I believed his weird stuff. But I really did get better at parallel parking. Like, right away!

I convinced the driving test instructor to let me play the tape, real softly, just during the parking part of the test. I passed. And he even said I was real mature for liking Cat Stevens and he hoped I understood the message of the music.

When I got home, I was thrilled about the two hundred dollars but also relieved that Dad would stop making me practice and yellin' at me from the passenger seat. He acted all proud and hugged me and kinda shook my shoulders a little. And then here's where it gets weird. He opened his wallet and took out this paper thing, and said, "Here you go. You earned this." And it wasn't two hundred dollars; it was a two-hundred-dollar travel voucher for United Airlines. I'm pretty sure I looked crestfallen, because he got a little indignant, and started tellin' me about how it was better than cash because it would encourage me to have an experience, and it was good for a lotta places with no blackout dates.

I took it and I was so mad, I stalked out to the Impala, and when I saw the dent in the back bumper, I got even more mad. I slammed the door good after I got in the car, and drove furiously out of the driveway. I turned up my Cat Stevens tape really loud and let his voice just drown out everything else. Pretty soon I was at the Asheville airport, and without thinkin' I just went inside. I think I left the car in the no-parking zone, and maybe with the door open, which Dad was probably pretty sore about later. I hope he got it back without too much fuss and trouble.

I marched up to the United Airlines desk and slapped that two-hundred-dollar voucher on the counter. The lady looked pretty surprised, but she asked me where I wanted to go. Then she showed me a list of all the places I could afford that still had flights goin' today. My choices were pretty slim. I stood at that desk for a long time, thinkin' about my dad and my sisters and the dent in the car, and all the stuff I seen and did over a long time just seemed to be going by in my mind. In the end I got the bright idea of provin' Shuggs right or wrong, and I figured I'd be able to let him know somehow. The lady was real nice when she explained that I was choosing a one-way ticket, not a return, and there was no changing or refunding once I made up my mind. I told her I wouldn't hold it against her.

When I got to heaven, it was real easy to find Allen Ginsberg. He was hanging out in a dingy bar just like the one we got in town, only I can drink now because there aren't really any age limits for alcohol and stuff. Or there aren't really any ages. I'm not sure. It's cool. Allen Ginsberg laughed a lot when I told him about Shuggs's idea, but he didn't deny it either. I was most surprised to find out that Cat Stevens isn't here yet, but they do have his music, so we're enjoying that and waiting for him.

March 2016

Character: A doppelgänger

Action: Sneezing

Setting: A marina

Prop: A roll of 2009 minted quarters

Stand In

Summer Olsson

She sat in the bar at Gino's, her third greyhound sweating rings onto the mahogany. Through the glass she could see the whole marina, all the drooping sailboats and staunch yachts blotting out most of the blue.

The bartender had already come by twice more, and she had gently rebuffed him. Normally she would have told a guy like that to fuck off and leave her alone, but her instructions were to not draw attention to herself. She sipped her drink with her sticky red lips and peeled her thighs off of the vinyl barstool to uncross and recross her legs. She fished her phone out of her bag. She only had ten more minutes to wait before the time was up and she could leave. In the beginning she thought this was kind of sexy and interesting, but it had turned out to be really boring. She'd been here for almost two hours. She decided she could take a quick bathroom break.

As she rounded the corner under the metal finger pointing the way to the "W.C.," she was hit from behind. What cracked against her skull was a roll of quarters, freshly minted in 2009, that had been picked up at a credit union that morning and would be dismantled and pumped into various pinball machines later that night. She did not know or care about this as her attacker dragged her unconscious body through a service door and into an alley. Blood trickled from the back of her head, but her long red hair caught it, mixed it into a sticky clot that never touched the floor. Luckily for her she didn't regain consciousness when her assailant dropped her behind a dumpster. Certainly he did her a favor when he shot her twice, once in the head and once in the chest, before he removed the ring finger on her right hand, which he pocketed to send to his employer later.

"Did it work? Is it over?" Eddie asked and then immediately sneezed. His allergies were really bad today. Dana knew she should feel sorry for him, but mostly she was annoyed. She was trying to concentrate. Looking through binoculars made her feel cross-eyed and gave her a headache. She pushed some red hair behind her ear.

"Yes. It's over."

"Thank god!" Eddie said and came up behind her. He put his long arms around her, pinning her arms and forcing her to lower the binoculars.

Dana relaxed against him. She breathed deeply a few times. Her shoulders lowered. For the first time in two hours, she was aware of the subtle rocking of the boat. Through the window in the hull, she could see gulls swooping to nip something off of the pier.

"I'll make some drinks," Eddie said. He went around behind the bar and took down two highballs.

She thought about how she and Eddie could watch birds now. They could sit on a beach somewhere without a constant buzz of tension. They could walk down the street in public somewhere—somewhere else, at least—without being terrified. Eddie handed her a drink. The first sip made her eyes tear up.

Dana wasn't going to say anything to Eddie about the near miss, but it was bugging her and she knew it would get worse. "I'm glad he sent someone else. I thought he would. But we really lucked out."

Eddie raised an eyebrow. "But she looked exactly like you. From a foot away, he would have been fooled."

She raised her glass toward him. "Yes, but she ordered the wrong drink. I only drink Manhattans."

April 2016

Character: A barber

Action: Parallel parking

Setting: At a bike rack

Phrase: "You gotta remember where you are"

Extinction

Laurel Rogers

The icy wind wrapped around Kay like a vicious sneer, as if the islands themselves knew how much she didn't belong there. Not now anyway. Not in this alternate timeline she'd lived for the past five aching years.

Bill's face was, as always, immutable, but that was preferred to the blood-red anger that had overtaken him when she pulled the car up by the bike rack in a haphazard version of parallel parking near the beach. "You still just can't do it, can you?" he fumed.

Well, fuck him.

The old Kay would feel the sting of his words. The old Kay, who had a heart that did more than beat.

A heart that stopped feeling years before.

You could only find a few references to it online, always tagged as the "Puget Sound Mini Tsunami." No one really knew much about it—almost know one ever heard of it.

But it was the lightning-rod moment for Bill and Kay. An extinction-level event, as tsunamis often were. And here they were at the spot, five years and a few months later.

Because coming on the anniversary would be cliché, Kay had said.

Too fucking impossibly painful, she meant.

Time supposedly heals all wounds, but it hadn't proved to have an effect on the abject, utter loss of an entire world. And that's what the "mini tsunami" had been—the Great Flood, ending of everything. Just a random late spring day, the kind when families play, lovers kiss, sailboats unfurl their spinnakers, and hillsides fifty miles away don't collapse into the sea, spawning a two-foot-high relentless, powerful ripple across the sound and around Spieden Island.

And funneled—"with surgical precision," one newscaster described it—right into the spit by Davis Head.

Where Bill and Kay were.

Watching.

Watching in utter helplessness as their three kids looked in momentary shock as the water receded to showcase the crabs and sea slime and purple clams they had, but seconds before, longed to reach under the too-deep water.

"Mom, look!" Lina hollered. "A starfish!"

It was the last thing Kay would ever hear any of her children say.

"You've gotta remember where you are," Kay's therapist reminded her about once a month. "And that's a lot further than you were last month."

Was it? Was it really? Because it felt like a treadmill. Day after day, going through the motions of a life Kay wouldn't wish on her worst enemy.

Bill was on a treadmill too. It just wasn't the same treadmill. And gradually Kay realized it wasn't even pointed in the same direction.

At first, there was still some kind of connection. The inconceivable grief, combined with a zombie-like onslaught of "helpful" opinions offered by friends and family, had given them at least the shared focus of survival.

No, they weren't wearing lifejackets, they answered a thousand times. *No, it wouldn't have occurred to them. How could we possibly know if it would've made a difference? NO, NO ONE IN THEIR RIGHT MIND WOULD PUT LIFE-JACKETS ON KIDS WADING IN ANKLE-DEEP WATER SO FUCK THE HELL OFF.*

Over time, the world went on. Other children died. A mom down the street died five weeks after being diagnosed with melanoma. Bill's grandpa died. A truck driver on I-5 fell asleep and took out a motorcyclist heading home from work.

Death was everywhere, and after a few months, Bill and Kay weren't special. Or interesting.

Or even alive, they realized.

But no one else really noticed.

Kay had heard of people "growing apart" or just "not having that spark" anymore. People got bored. People got lonely. People got scared as the years ticked by, closer to an unknown but certain doomsday looming—age seventy-two? Eighty? Maybe one hundred? No one knew, but it was there like a barber holding a straight-edge razor, ready to cull a few more strands from the world's tapestry.

But only three strands mattered to Kay, and they were gone. And over time, as she looked at Bill, he seemed more and more part of the memory of those family days—days that gradually became myth and legend, rolled up in the modern cave paintings of family scrapbooks.

And just as untouchable as an extinct mammoth.

Extinct. That was what their marriage was. They realized this quietly, she and Bill. Each on their own.

Out of habit she kissed him on the mouth on his way out the door to work for the first time since their world was destroyed. But there was nothing there. For either of them.

"It'll take time," the counselor assured them, first together, when they tried together, and then separately.

Gradually everything was separate. First, Kay tried a few nights on the couch, knowing too well her insomnia was keeping Bill from sleeping. "One of us has to get some rest," she said as she left their plush king-size bed.

She never came back, in word or deed.

And Bill never asked.

Extinct.

Coming back to Spieden Island again was Bill's idea. It wasn't a romantic proposition. They both knew that. They hadn't even driven together, although they decided to meet at the Anacortes ferry terminal and go that far together to save a few bucks. Naturally that was Bill's idea, but Kay knew, in fairness, it was best. Lawyers cost money. Tax accountants cost money. Never mind the therapy bills, the online dating fees, an increasing amount of money going out the door separately.

The papers were ready, and they both were fine. It didn't hurt, in the same way you don't feel a thing when they remove your leg while you're under general anesthesia. But they weren't macabre enough to make some grand ceremony of it on the island.

That wasn't the point.

Even though neither ever said it, Kay knew that this trip was a simple, quiet, strangely necessary funeral. A terribly cold one, inside and out.

Kay shivered again as she looked out toward Pearl Island. The Davis spit was so much the same—its swath of granite gravel and pearly clams. Million-dollar yachts still bobbed at moorages out of reach of the common folk. Yet it was oddly silent, shrouded in winter's inescapable solitude.

Kay was grateful. The island she had known and loved was seared in her memory, an endless summer where her children played happily in their eternal youth.

She looked at Bill, whose stoic face was lined with ever more wrinkles even if they weren't caused by grins and laughter.

Suddenly he looked at her, really looked at her, as if for the first time in all these years. And then he spoke aloud the epitaph they both had written in their hearts.

"I always thought I'd grow old with you."

Extinct.

May 2016

Character: A delivery person
Action: Taking x-rays
Setting: An ice rink
Phrase: "Heads-up"

The Disappearance
of Bobby Gond

Donald Carson

Everyone searched and searched, but they could not find him.

If ever a seven-year-old could have been said to have vanished, it was Bobby.

His grandmother, old Muriel Gond, who was raising Bobby after his mother had left town with a pizza delivery person Muriel referred to only as "that man," stomped all over the property, looking in old refrigerators, rusting car carcasses, and oil drums.

She pulled things off of shelves.

She clattered in the garage, in the barn, in the overhang where the big RV had been parked for ten years without moving an inch.

She yelled until she was hoarse.

And she was not alone. The entire town of Ice Rink, Idaho (pop. 837) roamed the streets shouting Bobby's name until the glow on the horizon disappeared and it was too dark to see. Many of them abandoned the search then, but a few of the brave flashlight owners got them out, dusted them off, and continued searching across the fields, rustling through the grass like a herd of migrating elk.

Muriel worried that Bobby had never spent a night out of his bed before and would be scared to be by himself in the dark. The matriarchs of the town comforted her as they sat up into the night, watching Fox News and waiting for their own news from the search parties.

Morning came. The sun rose, and the town rose, but no Bobby. Muriel Gond finally fell into a troubled sleep. She was a religious woman, and in a dream God came to her, pressed a cold cloth to her brow, and, in the voice of Charlton Heston, told her not to worry.

They never did find Bobby.

The search went on for several days. In the second week, it became half-hearted. In the third week, it was quarter-hearted, and so on, until there was no heart left at all.

It should be said, and here is as good a place as any, that Bobby was no ordinary boy. You only know him as a missing child, but to those who knew him, Bobby was a delight. Most young boys, you can take or leave. Mostly leave. They're noisy, smelly, and full of questions that don't need answering. The best you can say about seven-year-old boys is that they'll "probably turn out okay."

But Bobby was different. Smart, funny, and kind, he made everyone around him glad to see him show up and sorry to see him leave.

And when he disappeared from their lives so suddenly and mysteriously, the town of Ice Rink was forever more subdued after that.

Muriel took ill, with a fever, and raged and groaned and was on the verge of cursing God, but thought better of it. They needed his help to find Bobby. She grew no better, and finally the doctor took x-rays to see what was the matter. He could find nothing wrong.

But one day Muriel sprang out of bed, exclaiming that God had come to her in a dream and told her that all was accounted for. That was all she would say. But she never was quite the same after that, fading like wallpaper in the sun as the years went by.

And the years did go by. Muriel, who had been old when Bobby went missing, grew even older.

And then she died.

Muriel had been something of a hoarder, saving the possessions of her late husband, Josephus X. Gond, in careful stacks as though his life had been worthy of furnishing a museum.

After Bobby disappeared, she became even worse. Perhaps she thought that by saving everything that came into her life, she could somehow atone for having misplaced her grandson.

When she died, the town had a lot of sorting to do. The one Goodwill was strained to the bursting point with the detritus of Muriel Gond's home and many outbuildings.

Before he settled in Idaho, Josephus had been a cook in the Merchant Marine, and one of the things he'd brought back with him was the taxidermied corpse of an alligator perched on a rock, swatting at a stuffed kingfisher flying overhead on a wire. No one knew how Josephus had managed to get the ridiculously heavy thing from God Knows Where to his home, but he had. And it had the place of honor in the middle of the garage, where it had lain, gathering the dust of the ages, for half a century.

When it came time to take the alligator out of the place, it took seven men and a truck with a winch.

As they were dragging it into the yard, it came apart. Turns out the rock that alligator was on was hollow—who knew?

Someone yelled, "Heads-up!" at the man driving the truck, and he stopped tugging.

They all gathered around the rock that had split horizontally in two, showing the hollow space within.

Where the skeleton of a young boy lay, perfectly preserved, his empty eye socket pressed against a small hole in the rock, gazing eternally at the world outside.

No one could figure out how Bobby had gotten himself into the hollow of the rock without help, nor why no one had heard him yelling when they searched.

But there he was.

What was not widely reported, and only spoken of in hushed tones among the townspeople, was that the skeleton had grown small wings— just bones now—that curled against his body as he lay.

It couldn't be explained.

But anyhow, there is so much in this life that can't be explained, isn't there?

July 2016

Character: A diplomat

Action: Going viral

Setting: Before the revolution

Phrase: "Gotta catch 'em all"

Only the Lonely

Donald Carson

They call me a monster. And perhaps I am.

They call me a lover. And I do have my moments.

I do not think they suspect that in my large and fiery heart lies the spark of sensibility. To them, I am just a large lump. A thing to take advantage of until no more advantages remain to be taken.

They talk about leaving me. I would like to see them try! They have hurled themselves away from my massive body, but they always return, like fleas flick back onto a dying dog.

They give me no credit for creating them, and perhaps they are right. Perhaps it was not I who brought them into being, but something larger than myself. Perhaps there is a God.

I doubt it.

I was lonely. I longed for a mind to share my deep, dark cavernous thoughts with. And so I fiddled and I fidgeted. I sent lightning where lightning might not have gone. I crafted and I coddled. I was quite clever, if I do say so myself. Eventually things went viral, as they say now, and I sat back to watch.

It took a while, but I had a while. Fire burned, and cauldron bubbled.

And forth they came.

How they have disappointed me! I thought to have companions, but instead I have a mange that spreads across my skin, leaving death in its tracks.

And they think *me* a monster. Oh, I kill them casually enough, as one brushes a mosquito from one's shoulder or poisons ants. Gotta catch 'em all!

So I am a monster. But I am also a diplomat. I want them to one day be my equal, so I try to keep them alive, but I despair how long it will take. Or whether I will have to start over.

They are the humans I birthed in my wet womb. And I, I am the planet they call the Earth. Brooding, scheming, and always hopeful that someday I will meet my equal. Before the revolution that is intelligence spread across my surface, I had given up hope.

Now, I have a tiny particle of hope. Will they someday evolve into a companion for me?

Oh, I've reached across the emptiness and tapped Venus on the shoulder. I've called out to Saturn. But apparently I am the only sentient planet in hailing range.

And while they prattle, and dissect their minuscule existences, and give themselves hugs, and take selfies, I wait.

For a friend.

August 2016

Character: A reluctant volunteer

Action: Signing a contract

Setting: A housing development

Phrase: "You're not from around here, are you?"

Baltic Avenue

Melinda McCamant

Just a pretty girl from Baltic Avenue: I was awed, intimidated even, by his swagger, the way his teeth glittered when he talked, his bright hotels on Boardwalk.

"You're not from around here, are you?" he whispered in my ear, and I could feel the heat of his breath penetrate my brain, the bulge of brightly colored bills in his hand, a rainbow of promises.

And so I rolled the dice and we moved on, a jalopy and a top hat traveling the same path but seeing different sights.

He gambled, built hotel after hotel on credit and lies, not just Boardwalk but the railroads— even the lights and the water were his.

He had everything but Baltic Avenue. Baltic Avenue, a shadowy street lined with tiny green houses, was mine. Every time he came back around, he came back to Baltic Avenue, wooing me, promising the Atlantic's waves, promising a moon plucked and pitted from the sky.

I was tired and his light was so bright, but the moment I signed, the moment I said "I do," I knew I was just another pawn—a player in his game of rainbow money and plastic hotels.

But I still had Baltic Avenue, the scent of earth in our garden after a rain, the rumble of trains in a distant rail yard, the red bite of fruit, and my mother's kisses before she died.

It's a funny thing to get what you think you want: the last piece of cake, a diamond, a rich man, and realize that the getting was the good part, that the journey around the board was what made the game worthwhile. Not the houses, or hotels, or rainbow money. And not the glittery man who blows hot air but deflates at a touch and cannot read anything but his own name.

I was his dutiful wife; his get-out-of-jail-free card, his reluctant volunteer hostess, his volunteer whore.

At least I still have Baltic Avenue and one more roll of the dice.

October 2016

Character: A mechanic

Action: Listening to Bruce Springsteen on NPR
on *Fresh Air*

Setting: A church

Phrase: "It's just locker room talk"

Sanctuary

J. Turner Masland

The sun danced down through the sugar maple tree leaves already yellowing on an October afternoon and now seemed to be saturated with the late-afternoon light.

Jerry was walking up his five-mile driveway, which wound through some backwoods hills. He was walking back from the main road and his mailbox. Checking the post was how he justified his afternoon walks to his family: but in reality they were his afternoon devotions, his ritual to commune with the spirit. He replaced life with an institution with this mountain acreage, which has been his sanctuary for many decades now.

His greasy hands carried a few bills and some seed catalogs. Toby the golden retriever raced ahead, on the scent of some woodland creature. Jerry hitched up his sagging jeans and shuffled some pebbles out of his way. The cool mountain air and the breeze through the tree boughs brought him peace.

He crested a hill and rounded a corner and paused to take in the sight before him. Some cleared land, a full two acres of gardens, his garage, and an ancient farmhouse. His home: his pride and joy. Today it looked glorious bathed in the afternoon light with the trees in the distance just starting to turn. He'd left life as a minister, too fed up with the hypocrisies of the church and the fast-paced speed of modern life, to start his life as a mountain man. His children at the time were just toddlers and loved their new life of homeschool and exploring the woods. But after years of hard work and farm chores, their enthusiasm vanished and they all ran away as soon as they could. His sweet wife, Gertrude, though, has stood by his side through tough winters and bountiful harvests.

As he approached the house, he could hear Terry Gross's voice float across the homestead. Gertie insisted on the radio, one of the few connections to the modern world. It reassured her, while they lived their life off the grid, to have an umbilical cord of radio waves to know that the rest of humanity hadn't totally imploded.

Jerry threw the mail down on the porch, let Toby into the kitchen, and made his way to the garage. He rolled up his sleeves and started tinkering with the motor of his Ford pickup. With a

little ingenuity and a few old manuals, he managed to keep the old piece of shit running.

"How was your walk, hun?" He heard Gertie
approach the garage.

"Just fine, my darling. Who is Terry talking
to today?"

"Oh, she's interviewing that Bruce Springsteen.
Can you imagine? Seventy-five years old and just
released another album. This one protesting
Trump's second term. He called it *Locker Room
Talk*. Silly business, if you ask me."

"Silly, maybe. If Bruce ain't careful, he
gonna wind up under one of Chris Christie's
secret tribunals. Goddamn, how did this shit get
so fucked up?"

"I know, Jerry, I know. Any word from the
kids?"

Jerry looked up from the motor and shook
his head. Gertie knew not to get her hopes up,
but she just couldn't help it.

Starting before the 2016 election, when
things started to get real ugly, Jerry and Gertie
had begun their preparations. Stockpiling seeds.
Teaching themselves how to install solar panels.
Expanding their root cellars. Talking about getting some horses and donkeys to help with plow-
ing the fields.

When the unthinkable happened, and Trump took advantage of the missing Supreme Court justice to weasel his way into office through a contested election, they gave up on all electronic communication. Their kids thought they had finally lost it. They indulged their parents' letter writing at first but turned down their invitations to return to the farm. Soon the letters just stopped.

But Gertie and Jerry knew: the increased oil drilling, the alliance with Russia, the centralization of power, the mass deportations, the increased militarization, the occupation of Latin America were all signs of the end of times. Jerry may no longer be a minister, but he was still expecting the four horsemen to appear any day now.

"Come on, hun," Gertie prodded Jerry. "The sun tea is done brewing, and I have a new batch of mint balm for your shoulder..."

Jerry wiped his greasy hands on the back of his jeans and followed his wife to the house. The smell of smoke from the woodstove put some worries out of his mind, for the moment.

Jerry and Gertie spent the afternoon on the porch. He was helping her ball up skeins of wool, and Terry Gross's voice lulled him to sleep.

"Jerry... Jerry..." Gertie shook him awake.

"What, dear, what is it?"

"Listen," she said.

He looked out over the field, now blazed with pink and reds as the sun set behind the hills.

"Gertie, all I hear are the evening swallows chirping in the trees. It's a mighty peaceful sound."

"Exactly, Jerry. The radio went silent."

"You check the batteries?"

"We've been using the solar one, and it was fully charged."

Grunting, he got up and got the emergency radio down from the cupboard. He cranked it three, four, five times. Static. He walked over to the other radio, moved the dial up and down. Static. The radio had been on constantly, for years. Radio silence could mean only one thing...

Gertie's eyes pierced him. "It's time, Jerry. It's happening."

"I think you're right, hun. Let's get out the guns. Pray to the Lord we aren't going to need them. And pray to the Lord our children find their way back to us."

November 2016

Character: An Australian tourist

Action: Passing the salt

Setting: A beach resort

Prop: A hat pin

Terminal Encounters

Daniel Granias

Like bones, our hearts are strong, but also easily broken. Little did Amos Dickson, a forty-two-year-old truck driver from the great state of Texas, ever imagine that he would get tossed on a plane and sent to a beach resort in Sydney, Australia, by a gas company sweepstakes. Little did ChoYoo Park, an air hostess for Korean Air, know that the international terminal at Sydney Airport would run into their third week of union strike on the day of her last flight home to Seoul.

But there they were, three stools apart at the bar of the Applebee's between terminals A6 and A8. Amos was on his third beer, building up his liquid courage to leave the airport, entering the only other foreign land he'd set foot on besides Oklahoma. He first noticed the young Korean air hostess, her jet-black bangs pinned to the left and her red-and-blue Korean Air scarf tied elegantly to the right. It was mildly surprising that she ordered a margarita with extra salt. It was extra surprising that she drank it as a chaser to the two shots of tequila that were hiding behind it. "Pass the salt!" she whined in a sing-song sort of happy-angry familiarity. Amos slid the salt down the waxed oak counter, and upon receiving it, ChoYoo caught a glance at the lonely American.

Perhaps it was a result of watching a Korean-dubbed version of *Walker, Texas Ranger*, but between his denim shirt, his strong, bearded jaw, and his light blue eyes, there was something about his smile, the way his grin looked left while his eyes looked right into her dark umber wells. They stayed in their seats for the remainder of their drinks, but just as Amos made his way out of the bar, ChoYoo surreptitiously kicked her suitcase over from her barstool. Like a drunken show horse, Amos leaped into the air, kicked his legs out, but caught the handle of the mobile luggage and tumbled head over spurs.

Laughing together, ChoYoo helped Amos to his feet and he held her elbows, stabilizing himself against her polyester jacket. Amos looked at ChoYoo's eyes, but they were looking downward, directly in the central vicinity of his pants. Following her gaze, Amos noticed that his belt buckle had come undone and was hanging limp by one hinge. Giggling mischievously, ChoYoo took the pin from her folded pillbox hat holding her bangs in place and corrected the hinge, unabashedly grabbing Amos's belt in a full-fisted grip.

They were an unexpected pairing, like polka dots and plaid. East met west in the Great Down Under. They spent another two hours at the bar, learning about the other's homeland and what brought them to Australia. But just as they were about to leave the bar together, the A6 terminal announced the end of the international union strike, and all Korean Air staff were to report to their flights in the F-lines. Three other Korean Air hostesses appeared from the Applebee's out of nowhere, picked up ChoYoo's bags, and carried her away before she could look back at the lonely Texan.

Author Bios

Blythe Ayne, PhD, lives on ten acres of forest on the north side of the Columbia River near Portland, Oregon. She's an author, artist, and university instructor of writing and speech. Her written work has appeared in over one hundred publications. Along with her writing, her greatest commitment is to the stewardship and preservation of her forest, where wonderful and diverse flora and fauna thrive.

Donald Carson is a digital content strategist in Portland. He is a food addict and must eat at least three times a day to sustain a metabolic high. He enjoys avoiding things he knows he should do, working on the same novel for ten years, and tending to the needs of two furry animals that have taken up residence in his house.

Jenn Crowell is the author of the novels *Necessary Madness* (Putnam, 1997) and *Letting the Body Lead* (Putnam Penguin, 2002). At the time of her Mini Sledgehammer win, she was a student in the low-residency MFA program at

Antioch University Los Angeles and was at work on her third novel.

Kathleen Culla Valle has lived in six different states and is calling Portland, Oregon, home for now. She is a writing facilitator with Write Around Portland, because she loves writing. Kathleen has been journaling and penning stories ever since she can remember but has never actively sought publication. She has an MA in English education from Brooklyn College and is currently substitute teaching.

Jeremy Da Rosa is a writer, educator, and painter who currently lives in Colombia. He was born in Salinas, California, where lettuce and tomatoes come from.

Peter D'Auria was born and mostly raised in Portland, Oregon. He has worked as an amusement park ride operator, cheesemonger, reporter, and English teacher. He currently lives in Indonesia.

Sarah Farnham is a bicoastal wanderer. She loves writing, coffee, and sunshine. Poetry was her main squeeze until she accidentally started writing fiction. You can contact her at westcoastcharliedenver@gmail.com.

Kerrie Farris lives in Portland and watches the crows when she ought to be working.

Elisabeth Flaum began writing fiction because of *Doctor Who* and hasn't yet been able to stop. She lives in Portland, Oregon, where she works in accounting, races dragon boats, and writes poetry about volcanoes. Follow her ramblings at www.elisabethflaum.wordpress.com.

Lisa Galloway graduated from Pacific University's MFA in Writing program in 2007. She's a Pushcart nominee and author of the book of poetry *Liminal: A Life of Cleavage* (Lost Horse Press, 2011). A Northwest transplant, Lisa grew up in Indiana where she was adopted into a family with Southern Baptist roots—she contends that the Bible Belt still leaves welts.

Daniel Granias is a writer, teacher, and visual artist specializing in ceramic sculpture while living in Portland, Oregon. His writing practice has been regularly fueled by the Mini Sledge-hammer series since 2013, and he is forever grateful to its community for their undying enthusiasm and support.

Jennifer Gritt is the associate director of Pittock Mansion, a historic house museum in Portland, Oregon. A lover of history and literature, Gritt also has a background in feature article writing for magazines such as *Running Times* and *Wisconsin Outdoor Journal* as well as local newspapers. The Oregon Book Awards Mini Sledgehammer was Gritt's first fiction writing contest and win.

Pat Jewett received a fellowship with the AmericaWalks Walking College in 2017. She is busy learning about walkability in a four-month online course and mentoring group. She's looking forward to attending the National Walking Summit in September. Pat is attempting early retirement so that she can have more time to write, walk, and travel. She also owns a website, www.allthingswalking.com.

Originally from the Southwest, **J. B. Kish** moved to Portland, Oregon, in 2012. He spends his weekends in a walk-in-closet-turned-office working on novels. His newest, *A Wall for Teeth* *and Stingers*, was released in June 2017. He can be reached at jbkwriting@gmail.com.

Miriam Lambert is a physicist, a writer, and a lover of dogs, books, and chocolate. Her flash fiction "Night Delivery" is available in the *Baby Shoes* anthology (Browncoat, 2015), on Amazon.com, and wherever books are sold. You can find more about her books featuring physics, vampires, and Renaissance art at www.mslambertauthor.com.

Jack Mahaffy has two sons, and the older one—the one with the red hair—at age six, he said that what reading does is put magic in your head, and the other one—the younger one, and as it happens at an earlier age—said that every story is a flamed-out window with the face of a human, and of course the truth is that they were both right, my sons, and I live with them and with my wife and with the good old dog here in Oregon likely always.

Elizabeth Grace Martin is a writer, a creative, and a traveler. She fantasizes about Betty White being her soul sister, or at least grandma. She gives probably horrible relationship advice on her weekly podcast, *I've Only Been Wrong Twice*, and does writing with words at www.elizabethgracemartin.com.

J. Turner Masland is a librarian, currently working at Portland State University as the access services assistant manager. Originally from New Hampshire, he has lived in Portland since 2006. When not in the library, he enjoys hiking, swimming, taking trips to the coast, and working on his writing. You can learn more about him at www.masland.weebly.com or follow him on Twitter @deweysnotdead.

Melinda McCamant: reader, writer, photographer, recipe developer, food stylist. Sometimes there is travel, trails, friends, and wine. Find her work at www.melindamccamant.com and www.recipefiction.com.

Elissa Nelson, writer, teacher, and lover of life, died in 2013 at age thirty-seven, many years after being diagnosed with a brain tumor. She lived in Portland, Oregon, taught high school English, which she loved, and worked arduously on a novel. She produced two issues of a very small zine: *The Hundred Most*

Influential Writers in My Life to Date, As Best I Can Remember and Mostly Not Including Zines.

Barry Netzley's work has been published on the Mini Sledgehammer site, in *The Sun Magazine*, in the poetry anthology *Pay Attention: A River of Stones*, and as podcasts for the blind and print-impaired through the Audio Internet Reading Service of Los Angeles. He has also read his work aloud at the Vault Voices reading series. He credits the fun and talented folks he's met through Mini Sledgehammer, The People's Ink, and A Tribe of Writers PDX for sharpening his work. Barry's currently learning acoustic folk guitar while a pile of story drafts languish in the may-have-potential doldrums.

Summer Olsson is a writer, performer, and designer. She loves a great story, a tight deadline, or a funny wig. She is active in the arts community in Portland, Oregon, and beyond. Summer is one-half of the clown group Duo Doppio and the coproducer of the Portland Puppet Slam. She holds a BFA in theater from the University of New Mexico and is a graduate of Dell'Arte International School of Physical Theatre.

Laurel Rogers loves to make up stories. Sometimes she even realizes they're fiction. Other times she fashions them into website content, blogs, and twisted Facebook posts about her family. One day soon, she'll actually get her own blog going at www.theclockstruckmidlife.com.

Pam Russell Bejerano is a writer and educator who lives in Chico, California. Pam has written a novel set in Nicaragua; a chapter was published in *VoiceCatcher*'s winter 2016 issue, available at www.voicecatcherjournal.org. Pam has lived abroad several times, and she weaves multicultural issues and the strength of women throughout her writing. She is currently working on her third novel set in the mountains of Ecuador.

Jarrod Schuster: The author of this work, like that of any *good* author, is entirely implied. Feel free to grace him, her, or it with whatever characteristics, attributes, or opinions you may wish. Just do not be boring with your details. Everyone abhors a bore.

Courtney Sherwood is editor-in-chief of *The Lund Report*, a news website dedicated to covering Oregon health care data and policy. She's a volunteer stage manager for Portland's Wordstock book festival and part of the leadership team for the SOAK art and culture festival that takes place in Eastern Oregon each year. Courtney is also a competitive dragon boat paddler with Team Fusion and is a word nerd seeking to boost the prominence of written expression at Burning Man. She lives in Portland with her cat, Mister.

Fufkin Vollmayer worked as a journalist before kids and is finishing a memoir of the whole goofy enterprise known as single parenting, anonymous donor insemination, and having absolutely no idea on how to be a good mom owing to Really Terrible Parents (warning: alcoholism and mental illness and living in Reno, Nevada, are covered) in her upcoming book, *Because You Love Them Like Crazy*.

Acknowledgments

The production of this book was made possible first and foremost by Indigo: Editing, Design, and More. Editors Ali Shaw and Kristin Thiel cofounded the Sledgehammer Writing Contest. Thanks to their initiative to create such an effective platform, the miniseries continues to this day and has distilled into this anthology of winning writers.

Like the stories in this collection, the cast and crew of moderators for the Mini Sledgehammer Writing Contest series has been subject to prompts, current events, benchmark achievements, and, eventually, room for growth and moving on. After Ali and Kristin, other moderators have included Susan DeFreitas, a fellow Indigo editor and judge of Sledgehammers past. Courtney Sherwood brought Sledgehammer to Burning Man. Elissa Nelson's spirit will always be adored and sincerely missed. The next era of moderators introduced Daniel Granias, John Cartier, J. Turner Masland, and Jeremy Da Rosa, and now Summer Olsson, Sarah Farnham, Donald Carson, and Laurel Rogers have stepped up to the prompting plate.

None of these stories could have been written if not for a space in which to scribble and scramble. Andy Diaz and the staff of Blackbird Wine & Atomic Cheese always keep a table open for us and continue to give generously month after month. Other hosts have included Néna Rawdah at St. Johns Booksellers, Susan Moore and Literary Arts, Cloud and Leaf Bookstore, Metlakatla Community Library, Sweet Pea Baking Company, Floyd's Coffeeshop, Third Street Books, and Burning Man.

In the years that Mini Sledgehammer has been in operation, countless writers have felt the pressure of thirty-six minutes. The variety of stories in this book are a thin slice of the people who sat at the table—some only once, some for a stint or two, and others who stuck around. Several of those faithful returners became moderators, and some of those moderators became curators, editors, designers, event planners, and publicists for this anthology—all on a volunteer basis. Special thanks to Jeremy, Daniel, John, Turner, Summer, Sarah, Donald, and Ali for their contributions, and Hana Hiratsuka for donating the cover design. We couldn't have produced this anthology without any of you.

Event Information

Mini Sledgehammer Writing Contests are still going strong! If you're in the Portland area, we invite you to come check them out.

Mini Sledgehammer 36-Minute Writing Contest
Second Tuesdays
Blackbird Wine & Atomic Cheese
4323 NE Fremont St.
Portland, Oregon
6:30–8:30 p.m.

Read each month's winning story, including the archive, at www.sledgehammercontest.com.